Adrift

Adrift

a novel

LOREN EDIZEL

We acknowledge the support of the Canada Council for the Arts for our publishing program. We also acknowledge support from the Government of Ontario through the Ontario Arts Council.

Canada Council   Conseil des Arts   ONTARIO ARTS COUNCIL
for the Arts   du Canada   CONSEIL DES ARTS DE L'ONTARIO

Cover Design: Ingrid Paulson

Library and Archives Canada Cataloguing in Publication

Edizel, Loren
    Adrift : a novel / Loren Edizel.

ISBN 978-1-894770-73-6

    I. Title.

PS8609.D59A69 2011   C813'.6   C2011-903254-6

Printed in Canada by Coach House Printing

TSAR Publications
P. O. Box 6996, Station A
Toronto, Ontario M5W 1X7
Canada

www.tsarbooks.com

Dec 20, 2011

To my dear Going
With my best wishes,

Loren

Prologue

I THINK I SHALL ATTEMPT TO WRITE THE STORY of the old suitcase. A dusty brown leather suitcase sitting in the furnace room, an object that's been used for a long time, and passed down a few generations; it has old-fashioned angular corners, and there's a faded smell of leather on the outside; inside it has a shiny yellow lining thinning in parts, with matte jacquard flowers; it is slippery to the touch. Such a story may be worth telling: the various hands that wrapped around its worn handle, the movements of life it accompanied, the hopes and despair it witnessed of people long gone from memory.

When I inherited this ancient suitcase from my mother, I could not possibly have imagined that one day it would accompany me on my own escape into a new life. But that day arrived and I packed my few belongings into it and boarded a plane to Montreal. A feeling of vulnerability churned my guts as I gazed out the window of the aircraft, suspended above clouds. The stopovers in foreign airports only added layers to my sense of departure. Finally, a stamp on a passport page. The smell of fresh ink. I reached over to pick up my suitcase from the conveyor belt, a small duty-free bag swinging clumsily around my wrist getting in the way. Its odd occupant, a small jade statue of Buddha, a goodbye gift given hurriedly before my departure. It was 4:15 PM in Montreal, a new time on a new continent, suddenly six hours before the time on my wrist watch. The weight of the hard-edged suitcase bleached my knuckles. I knew fear all too well; but the sensation of having been ripped away was new. I wondered if anyone at the airport could see how raw I felt as the escalator moved me up into sunlight in search of a taxi.

Room 415 pushes the emergency button by her bed and waits. A few minutes later, John, the male nurse, saunters in. His black mane is shiny and like a folded crow wing flaps sideways on his creased forehead. He is not much taller than a young teenager, a metre and seventy-six at most, and his frame seems to carry more bone than flesh.

"You've buttoned it wrong," she points at his white uniform jacket and smiles, her crooked arm hanging midair.

"I was in such a rush to visit you!"

"Do you run as fast to all the girls here?"

"You can't hold that against me, dear. But I'm here now, at your service." He rubs his eyes a little to adjust to the light by her bed, before expertly folding back the covers to reveal her thick white legs, side by side, inert. He pulls a pair of latex gloves from the box on the tray beside her and puts them on. They smack as he adjusts them around his wrists.

"What does your wife say about your spending night after night around so many women lying in bed?"

"Can you do something for me? Turn your body to the left. Slowly. Perfect, thank you. She doesn't say much. Do you think she's got someone visiting her while I'm here?"

She nods thoughtfully. "You got kids?"

"Four."

"All at home?"

He nods.

"I wouldn't worry too much, then."

He smiles as he rolls up the sheet towards her middle, her back turned to him.

"How old are they?"

"Twelve, ten, eight, one."

"Lost count at the end, didn't you?"

"Sort of . . . This side is done." He unfurls the new sheet, the soiled one now in a rolled tube by her body. "I'll move to the other side and you'll be done in a second."

"Thank you. You're cheerful even in the middle of the night."

On the other side of the bed, he nudges her gently so she rolls over to the fresh sheet, and he repeats the same drill as before.

"All done."

He pats her shoulder and bunches up the soiled sheet and throws it into the cart. Finally he sprays the air freshener, in a quick automatic gesture.

"I'll see you later, then. Sleep well."

She smiles and closes her eyes.

e͡

He pushes the cart out to the corridor. It's painted a light green, the doors on either side left ajar, opening into neat quadrangular boxes. He is reminded of the less renovated parts of the hospital, with their arches and wooden doorframes, shady corners and dusty radiators. "We do prefer boxes," he ponders out loud as he pushes the trolley down the corridor, with its moans, snores, and whispers.

e͡

During night shift patients behave differently. When the sun begins to set, especially in winter, people confined to their beds grow restless. Their pains get worse, and the looming darkness is a reminder of the worst thing that could happen to them. The worst happen in the middle of the night, so they lie sleepless until they see the sun rise in the horizon from their window, the feeble orange light enabling them to sleep as they hold on to the hopes of a new day. Anyone who has not spent time in a hospital does not know the crucial difference between day and night. This is a secret he shares with all his patients. He goes to sleep in bright daylight, the way they do, and awakens in the dark to help them greet another day. Some don't make it through the night.

e⌒

Room 419 did not ring her buzzer. Her room is dark; through the window the city lights are visible, flickering in the distance. In between there and here round the mountain runs the forest like a black belt. He tiptoes inside to draw the curtains shut.

"Leave them!"

Startled, he turns toward the bed where the seventeen-year-old is sitting, knees drawn to her chest.

"Two more hours to sunrise," she says.

"And what are you doing up so early?" he half-scolds.

"My dad . . . " her voice trails off.

"Huh?"

"He didn't come to visit me."

"He wouldn't come at this hour of the night, dear. I'd go to sleep if I were you. He'll probably come tomorrow during the day."

She looks at him through the darkness. It sends a shiver down his spine, this look.

"Are you hurting somewhere?"

She shakes her head as she lies back and pulls the cover to her chin.

"That's better," he closes the curtain, "this will help you sleep, kid, and don't argue with me. Do you want water, anything else?"

She shakes her head.

"Good night, then." He walks out quietly.

"He always comes around this time . . . "

"Who? Your dad?"

"Hmm."

"No visitors allowed."

"He does."

"Yeah, you mean in your dreams . . . Well, then, close your eyes and wait for him."

He waves at her from the corridor and pushes the trolley down to Supplies to discard the soiled laundry.

 e

His packsack is a faded dark blue and the leather trimmings shine from age. He opens it to take out a sandwich wrapped in waxed paper. The bread is plain white, and between the white squares are squeezed a piece of mortadella and a slice of processed cheese the colour of egg yolk. He reaches in for his yogurt, apple, and cereal bar, and carefully lines them up on the desk. Nurses walk in and out the soundless swinging doors of a ward farther up. Chewing a corner of the sandwich he rummages through his packsack. An image flits through his mind of quartered crusty bread and sardines, a meal from long ago, bought from a rocking boat, eaten standing at the edge of the water. The smell of wetness everywhere. The horn of a ship passing. His teeth sink into a piece of mortadella.

"Hey John," calls out a passing nurse, smiling, "mortadella sandwich, again?"

"How did you guess?"

"Let's see . . . 'cause you've eaten the same thing for the last ten years? Before that, I don't know, I wasn't here, was I?"

"Anne of Green Gables, I bet there is something you do the same way every day."

She pauses to think. "Not food-related, that's for sure . . . " She waves vaguely before rushing on.

Her name is Anne. Not the slim, fiery redhead from Prince Edward Island. Brown hair, glasses, triangular shoulders, endomorphic softness all around. But she is from the Maritimes and likes the nickname, for the fiery redhead within, probably. He continues to search in his bag until he finds the pen. He takes it out and reaches for the bright green notebook.

e∽

He sits chewing and staring at the white page for a while. Turns to the previous page where his sprawling blue handwriting has leaked over the borders. He leans over to smell the inky page, then turns it and smells the blank one. Anne returns to fiddle with an IV pole behind the counter.

"How is the diary going?"

"It isn't a diary, I told you already."

"Then what is it?"

"Stuff . . . " He looks at her. "My thoughts for the day."

"That makes it a diary, John."

"I know what a diary is . . . It starts with a date, then goes 'Dear Diary, I met a handsome boy in my class today and I love him.' It's for schoolgirls. This is different!"

Anne is smiling. "How?"

"Just different, that's all."

"Am I annoying you?"

"Hmm."

She's fixed the IV pole and wheels it away.

"I'll leave you to your Thoughts of the Day, then. So long!" Her smile lingers on her face as she hurries down the soft vinyl tiles in her white shoes. He sees that they have taken the shape of her bunions, denting inwards at her big toes. Toes the shape of question marks. He wipes the crumbs off his lap and starts eating his yogurt, staring at his blank page. Yesterday, he couldn't write fast enough; today he has no words. Room 415 thinks he has a wife and children. So now they will all think he has a wife and four children, and ask him why he's never said anything about them all these years, why he doesn't bring them to Christmas parties. He will have to find names for them, schools. His wife . . . Where did he meet her—here or elsewhere? He smiles, picturing his entire brood dining on square mortadella sandwiches. Children wearing Salvation Army clothes, wife in plaid skirt with flowery blouse. Her black hair tied back into a flabby ponytail. Her eyes misty, as of so many women he sees on Bus 144. Her coat, a dull purple dating back to the early nineties,

7

with enormous shoulder pads. She sits close to the driver, to see the road, not to miss her stop. Her English is still broken after all these years, and her French, worse. She has not acclimatized to the cold. Thick grey woollen socks peek out from under her boots. She has worn them as a precaution, on top of her nylons, even though it is five degrees above zero, because you never know in this country. Her eyes veil the untold stories of another world, tales of all the regrets and of being reduced to a ghost. She works at a deli on Queen Mary; slicing sausages, bread, cheese. She slices, weighs, and wraps all day long, quietly, economizing on sounds. Her boss, Mr Benedek, likes to pat bottoms. Sheila, the eighteen-year-old cashier in tight pants gets patted a few times a day. Sheila does not say anything. Nobody says anything. When it happens, there is an embarrassed look on the women's faces. They are ashamed to be there, to be women, and ashamed for the boss.

"I swear I'll slap his hand, next time," hisses Sheila through her teeth as John's wife wraps wieners in brown paper.

"Why not . . . this time?" she asks Sheila in her halting English.

Sheila does not know the answer. His imaginary wife nods, as if she understands, and continues wrapping.

He has gone through the yogurt and the cereal bar and now hears the buzzer. The page is still blank. He closes the notebook and puts it into his packsack. He rises and walks to Room 417, where lies the old man who curses in lieu of speaking. "Fuck this shit . . . ," he whispers. "This fucking bed and these useless legs!" The man looks at John, who helps him get up in his bed, pulling down his parchment-skinned feet, and with his free hand grabbing the walker. The man puts his hands on the walker and one, two, three he pulls him up from the waist and off they go, rolling towards the bathroom, very slowly, the man pushing the walker. John helps him onto the toilet and leaves the bathroom, waits outside for a sign. The trickle of pee dribbles and finally stops, and John hears the old man groan, "Goddamn!" and knows it is time to enter. He returns him to bed and the old man lets himself almost fall on the pillow with relief. "Fucking hell!" John leaves the room as the night slowly retreats, and the sun splatters purple and red onto the eastern skies.

Once again he imagines his family. His wife's name is Selma. He sleeps while she works and vice versa. They have had this arrangement for some time, meeting for a few fleeting moments before one goes to bed and the other to work. The children are at school. He makes a note about finding out their names. They learn French, of course. Québécois French. He is not in the mood to invent a life for them this morning. He returns to his desk, his imaginary wife's name on his mind, causing some heartache.

℮ↄ

It is time to leave. The sun has risen, filling the ward with assorted sounds. As he hurries down the corridor he peeks into Room 419; the teenager sleeps profoundly, her arms limp on the twisted covers. When he reaches the main door, the patients disappear from his mind. The smell of brewing coffee and margarine on toast reaches him from the cafeteria by the entrance and he steps out into the waking city. It is 6:30 AM. Patches of black ice gleam along the edges of the sidewalk. He crosses the street and heads towards the bus stop.

On Bus 144 going east towards the Sherbrooke metro station he spots the Asian lady sitting at her customary seat by the window. She is always on this same bus, which is half empty at this hour, clutching a brownish red cloth bag with an embroidered dragon on it, her white hair wound tightly into a bun. The Asian lady gets off at St Lawrence, shuffling down the cold street as the bus moves away.

He gets off at the corner of Henri-Julien and Pine. As he unlocks the old wooden door to his triplex he is hit by that familiar winter smell: old newspapers, socks, stale cooking. There is a small window on the right side of the door beside his desk and bookshelves. He parts the blind slightly to look across the street. He waits a while. The door to the ground-floor apartment opens to release a woman with long wavy hair. It's hard to see her face or figure, covered as she is in layers of clothing and a scarf. Behind her comes a small boy, five years old at most, carrying a small bright-coloured packsack and bundled up so that only a wisp of blond hair is visible. She locks the door and they hurry towards the subway, hand in hand. He releases the blind and goes to his bedroom, removing his clothes on his way.

His night begins inside the dark room while the sun illuminates the frigid world outside. He closes his eyes thinking of a boat about to leave for the open seas, fish nets sitting in a humid pile. He observes the artfully curved wooden planks, freshly painted; the bottom black, the top half green, half blue with a yellow stripe running through the middle. The boat has a name which he cannot see. A fisherman works the oars in the still water as it slowly leaves the shore. He sees the man only from the back, his curls stiff from the salt. The strident cries of seagulls drown the creaking of the oars. He fades.

The woman from across the street is returning home minus the child. Her chin tucked down, she looks upset, cheeks wet with tears. He wants to rush out to help her. By the time he puts on his coat, hat, and boots, she has disappeared. He slams the door, cursing, and wakes himself up in his darkened room. A door has just slammed shut in the apartment upstairs, the sound still echoing in his ears. There is a school at the corner of the street and the kids leave in great numbers, noisily, a cloud breaking into rain, small voices pattering on his windows. "Children's voices rain and chime." He will write it down in his green notebook later. As he slowly rises, the inevitable loneliness of someone awakening while the world passes by descends upon him. He wonders if this is something carried into life from birth. You are born alone, silent, into a world that bustles with noise. Perhaps, he thinks, newborns cry to end their unbearable solitude. It is an old feeling and he has built his life around it. He stares at the armchair on which he threw his shapeless trousers as he rushed to bed. He goes to the kitchen feeling left behind as the school children go away, chiming. He sits at the kitchen table drinking coffee, reentering the space of his home. "Space becomes mine only when I have tamed it." He takes out his green notebook from his packsack, opens it, and writes the thought down. "Everything is strange at all times, until we tame it with our senses." He crosses out "we," replaces it with "I." He wonders which of the senses does most of the taming. "But the images in my mind, what is it they tame?"

e‿

His least favourite smell in the house is the one that wafts out from the fridge as he opens the door to take out his breakfast. A refrigerated broccoli smell along with sliced bread and cheese. He has another thought about the obsession with squareness. For something to appear neat, must it also come in a square? The bread, the toaster, the cheese to fit the sandwiches, and the bologna, the ham, and so on. He marvels at this train of thought, which first came to him in the hospital as he left the room of the woman in Room 415. Who thought up the idea that squares are good for the eye? Was it a baker? An architect? A picture framer? Did it simultaneously occur to a number of people, who then invented objects in that shape? Had the thought always been there, waiting to be discovered? He nods to himself as he spreads butter on his toast. *This thought is going nowhere.* But he notes it down in his book. An image comes to him, as he writes about squares, of an oval breakfast table, crisp white linen with blue flowers, a pot of apricot jam, brown tea in two glasses, slices of thick crusty bread, shrivelled black olives, a slab of soft, humid cheese glimmering in the early morning light, on a balcony facing the sea. The air is cool and dewy. The bats who fly zigzags over the harbour have disappeared, along with the mosquitoes. A young woman in a white bathrobe and dainty slippers, her copper hair rolled into a careless bun held together with a pencil, walks in and out making sure the table is set. He is leaning over the railing, his face tender from shaving. In the distance the ferry makes its way across the bay. The woman's eyes are fixed on the table. This could be any morning, and she could be alone. Her manner indicates this with a stubborn defiance. She doesn't look up as she says, "It's ready. Sit down." The wrought-iron chairs screech on the tiles as they pull them out to sit. At the side of the balcony a large clay pot holds bright red geraniums with tired-looking dusty leaves.

"You smell good," she says now, buttering her bread. He reaches quietly and squeezes her knee.

"Hmm . . . " She looks up at the sea and takes a bite of bread.

"I'd like to take a picture of this breakfast table with me."

"Whatever for?"

"Look at the shapes and colours here in the morning light. And the sea there," he waves an open hand across the blue expanse, "and you, with the pencil in your hair . . . I want to keep this . . . Where did you find these little slippers? They look like Cinderella's, all satiny and feathery . . . " An affectionate smile spreads across his face as he places his hand around the nape of her neck.

"You know I won't wait for you."

"I do." His hand slides away from her neck and back to the table.

"Good." She puts her bread on her plate and then, holding her forehead in her hands, she weeps quietly. She pushes away his hand when he tries to console her. Then she gets up, a slipper in one hand, and hurls it down the balcony with all her might. "There's your slipper!"

It stands, upright on the sidewalk, having missed the sea by about ten centimetres. He wants to laugh but she's too mad. A passerby has stopped in his tracks and is looking up. He goes and picks up the slipper hesitantly, turns it around in his hands and puts it back down before walking away, shaking his head.

"If you had thrown both down, he would have taken them to his wife," John tells her.

"Eat your food," she orders, wiping her tears on one sleeve.

"I cannot stay," he says, "and you say you cannot come with me. So what is there to do?"

"You're leaving me."

"No. You're not coming with me. You've chosen all this over me."

"Just finish your breakfast and go."

e⌐

He takes a bite of his square toast and chews it mechanically. *"On a street called Henri-Julien,"* he writes and puts down the toast, pushing aside the plate. *"I picked up your white slipper."* The poem is coming to him, pell mell, the page emptying his heart, word by impossible word. He writes and scratches and writes again and throws the pen across the room. Not long after this gesture of frustration, he remembers that it is his only pen and goes to look for it across the kitchen, under the furniture, finds it, and hooks it on his green notebook after blowing the dust off its surface.

Laundry needs to be done, he remembers, and stuffs his dirty clothes into a black plastic bag and leaves the house in a hurry, jacket unbuttoned and without gloves. The laundromat is two blocks away. He won't feel the cold until he is there, and once inside, his hands will painfully thaw as he places them on top of a dryer. The woman from across the street is there too, with her son. The boy is looking through the pages of a colourful book with a serious expression while she loads the dryer. She has three machines on the go. He quickly separates his clothes in two groups and starts the cycle. They are all sitting on the bench now, he, the woman, and her son. Her hair is twisted and pinned to the scalp with a large clip. The red dress hugs her figure all the way down to her knees and from there her black stockings go all the way into her dainty ankle boots. Quite arresting, this look, he thinks. He wants her to stand up and go to the machines so he can watch her move again. She is sitting, leg over knee, reading the newspaper, her bright red lips in a serious pout. Her long silver earrings take a swing whenever she moves. They would have looked gaudy on someone else, but with her, you just want to look at the blood-red dress hugging her small curves and everything else is there to promise more. The grey-haired man from down the block with his two huge dogs walks in with a small bag. He is always walking those dogs while his girlfriend jogs around the city. His loyal companions notoriously defecate while crossing streets, or nosing around bushes. "They can't hold it back; too old . . . ," he apologizes as people raise their

13

eyebrows, but he won't scoop, on account of the droppings being too soft. So they wait for a shoe to slide on them. The dog man has entered without his dogs, coffee mug in one hand and bag in the other. He stops in his tracks when he sees the woman; like a man having a heart attack he puts the hand with the bag to his chest, and remains that way for a moment, looking theatrical. She looks up from her newspaper nonchalantly, sensing the stillness all around, and sees him. She offers half a smile and a nod before going back to her newspaper. Leonard, the greying dog man, is not about to let her attention stray.

"Hi, neighbour!" he says, "how are ya?"

"Fine, thanks," she responds curtly without looking up.

"And you little guy, what's up?" He leans over the small boy with a smile. The boy nods and returns to his book, intimidated.

"Kinda boring to sit here and wait, eh?" The man sits down beside the boy and takes a sip of coffee.

The mother stops reading and glances at the man sideways, annoyed.

"What's in that bag?" asks the boy.

"Oh yeah, my smelly laundry . . . I should wash it, shouldn't I?"

The boy nods, the mother smiles. Leonard gets up to empty his bag into a washing machine.

His mother also gets up, checks the state of her laundry in the dryer and urges the boy to get up. "We have to go home now," she says, "we'll come back later."

The boy gets up, she helps him with his jacket quickly as she tries to wear hers and they rush out. The way she walks makes John want to drop everything and follow her. She sways her hips, but the movement is not enough to look deliberate. It's more like a small, hesitant pause on each side as she steps forward, as if she's not sure she should go on, creating an almost imperceptible awkwardness that charms the eye. His heart sinks at being alone in the laundromat now with Leonard, who looks quite disappointed as he returns to the bench to his coffee. John opens his green notebook and starts writing about the red dress, the awkward sway, the pout, and the silver earrings. The two men remain seated silently on the bench before the tumbling drums of the dryers, one holding a cup, the other writing in his notebook.

"Are you a writer?" Leonard asks after a while.

"No," John replies and continues to write.

"Oh!" Leonard says, shaking his head up and down. "I thought you were . . . I know this other guy who comes here and he is a writer. He does the same thing like you. His pen is more expensive though . . . " He gazes at the cheap ballpoint scribbling across the page.

"I see," John says vaguely. He stops writing. "Well, I'm not a writer. I'm just writing some thoughts down."

"Like a diary?" smiles Leonard, looking smug.

"No, not a diary. Just thoughts . . . "

"I have a lot of thoughts, but I don't write them down." Leonard looks ready to expound a theory.

"It's okay, man."

John looks down at his notebook, signalling the end of the conversation. Leonard takes another sip of his coffee and looks out the door. Two cops are standing outside the laundromat talking to a dishevelled man. Suddenly they push him down flat on his stomach and handcuff his hands at his back. One cop kicks the man in the side. The other one grabs him by the collar and lifts him up. The man's body hangs like a sack from the cop's hold. The other cop grabs the man's arm and they shove him into a police car and drive off.

"Did you see that?" Leonard turns to John.

"What?" John looks up.

"The cops . . . They just picked up a homeless guy as if he were a criminal. Just now, outside the window here." He stands up and goes to look out in disbelief.

He turns around. "Don't tell me you missed the whole scene?"

"I haven't seen anything . . . didn't even know there was a homeless guy standing there."

Leonard is shaking his head. "I can't believe they did that!"

"Maybe he was a pusher," suggests John.

"He looked pretty defenceless to me . . . He's one of the guys who sit on a bench in Carré St-Louis and have drunk conversations all day. I bet you've seen him before."

"I don't know."

"These cops . . . I tell you," starts Leonard, ready to begin a tirade against the doughnut-eating force, when John interrupts swiftly, "I need to go get something, I'll see you around!"

℮

He stuffs his notebook in his packsack, puts his laundry in a dryer, and quickly inserts some coins to start the machine. He will disappear for forty minutes, then return to collect his clothes. Leonard is the sort who will talk incessantly, walk you to your house, enter it uninvited, sit down, request a coffee and only leave when his jogging girlfriend returns home from work. That could easily be an entire day. John suspects this has happened to many in the neighbourhood. The solution is to not give him any opportunity.

As John leaves the laundromat he throws a glance sideways at Leonard, who sits pensive, watching the dryers turning while sipping what must be frigid coffee. As he rushes down the street and around the corner to Carré St-Louis, hands in pockets, packsack swinging around his left shoulder, he thinks about the beautiful neighbour. He hopes he'll run into her on her way back to the laundromat. He'll try to start a conversation. Perhaps, "Hi! We're neighbours . . . " That sounds pathetic. Perhaps, "Good afternoon. Did you know I live across the street from you and watch you daily as you come and go?" Frightening. He continues rehearsing his greetings as the park, surrounded by quiet, residential streets, seeps into his vision from the left. A soft whiteness covers the benches, tree branches, pond. There is snow everywhere, he realizes, it must have come down stealthily while he was in the laundry. His feet have left marks all the way from around the corner, like a squirrel's. Nothing moves in the park, hushed by the weightless blanket of snow. Its ornate old fountain towers aimlessly over the white pond. The sky

moves around in dark grey plates, interrupted by skeletal tree branches
thrusting upwards. He feels his nose and eyes water from the cold as he
walks towards his apartment. Such moments call for a magnificent love
affair, he muses. The beauty of this snowy park requires a story to be
weaved through it. He smiles, thinking of the dark-haired neighbour in
her fine ankle boots, taking small, trotting steps around the park, with
breathless Leonard chasing after her, still holding his coffee mug, his
Great Danes defecating on the pristine snow as they follow, hoping for
acknowledgement, a nod, a flirtatious smile; all in vain. "A truly exquisite
story," he tells himself, "a story that involves me."

He turns the key, unlocks the squeaking front door and leans on it
having closed it, breathing deeply. He takes off his track shoes in a hurry
and goes to the small window, parting the blinds to look at the neighbour's yellow door in the grey stone building. It has a small window
beside it, identical to his, and he wonders what lies on the other side of
the blinds. He can hear his heartbeat from within his ears, as he waits
for the yellow door to open and for her to reappear. The snow has
started falling again; tiny flakes moving haphazardly in the air, refusing
to touch ground before making a few flourishes. He feels happy to be
indoors, looking out the window to see the snow, the grey stones, the
yellow door, the black iron gate, the cars covered in white, and the
French municipal traffic instructions in red and black, saying something
like, "Park here between 3:00 AM and 9:00 AM but not between 9:00 AM
and 3:00 PM and not on the left side on Mondays and Wednesdays, and
not on any side without a permit, etc., etc., in fact, park anywhere if you
wish, because you will get a parking ticket no matter what you do."
Parking tickets already on the cars covered under thick snow. He smiles,
he would never move from this apartment, for the pleasures afforded
by this small window beside his door. The yellow door across the street
is pulled inward now, but no one appears for a while. He stares at the
dark space, his heart agitating in his chest. Then the brown wavy locks
spill out ahead of the woman. The boy follows, his hat shoved on his
head sideways, his feet still not entirely settled in the thick arctic boots.

He tiptoes up the few steps, and once on the sidewalk gives each foot a push down, running off to the side to gather snow. They are walking towards the laundromat. John rushes to his door, putting on his boots this time, much like the little boy, not bothering with the laces, which have never been undone, tiptoeing around in search of keys, gloves, and toque. He waits before opening the door, to allow the woman to turn the corner before rushing out, wet snow hitting his squinting face as he locks his door.

He hurries down the street towards the laundromat, hoping not to see Leonard of the Great Danes there.

Through the window he sees her folding clothes methodically at the table. She has not removed her coat and is no longer wearing the tantalizing red dress and ankle boots. He can see the legs of the grey sweatpants extending from underneath the coat, and thick winter boots around her ankles. Leonard of the Great Danes is absent from the picture. He walks in to the chime of the door. She offers a smile.

"It isn't dandruff!" He smiles back as he brushes off the flakes.

"Now there's something to be grateful about!"

He nods, amused, and goes directly to his dryer to check the state of his laundry. He shuts the door, letting the dryer continue to tumble noisily. He has not brought his packsack, or his notebook, having left in such a hurry, and feels awkward now as he goes to the bench to sit down. The boy has taken out a toy car from his pocket and is racing it up and down the wall. John observes the woman discreetly. She makes separate piles of the child's undershirts, underwear, sweaters and pants, and hers. He sees her hands expertly fold a few cotton thongs and shove them discreetly between two piles, same as her bras. It gives him a jolt to catch glimpses of her underwear, now imagining her small curves under the red dress in these small bits of pastel cloth. He feels his face heating up and turns to look out the window. When he looks back at her, she is folding sheets and pillowcases. From her method, he infers she is clever.

Then he realizes he had already determined superior intelligence from the way she looked at Leonard of the Great Danes earlier. It is not an entirely objective IQ indicator, and aware of his bias, he tries to understand how he has arrived at such certainty about her mind. Can a person's gait give something away? Or her pout? Or the sidelong glance? Perhaps the movement of her hands . . . she picks up his gaze which has remained locked on her hands folding the towels. He tries to conceal his embarrassment with a smile and hears his own voice say, "You fold your laundry very efficiently."

"Oh?" her lips curve upwards with a tinge of mockery.

He smiles, nods, and rises to go back to the drier to take out his clothes, which are not entirely dry, calculating that her folding efficiency would get her out of the laundromat in a few minutes. He wants to be ready. He takes his pile of clothes to the table next to hers and starts folding quickly. He stacks up his crumpled tee-shirts and shoves his boxers into his black garbage bag quickly, all the while stealing glances at her hands, which are now opening up her three heavy-duty green garbage bags before proceeding to carefully place the folded laundry inside. He has to time his speed so as not to be ready before her. They finish gathering their laundry at the same time and she tells her son to zip up his jacket as she hauls the first garbage bag over her shoulder. He interjects at this point, offering to carry the other two.

"My own bag is quite small compared to yours," he says, "I can carry your two other bags for you. I think we live on the same street . . . "

At first, she objects politely, saying she does this every week and is quite used to it. He insists that it is the least he can do, and she asks him where he lives.

"Henri-Julien," he replies.

"We do live on the same street. But I've never seen you there . . . "

He picks up her bags and they leave together.

"It's probably because I work shifts. I'm usually there when no one else is," he explains with a smile. "But I have seen you before. In fact, I think you live right across from me."

The look in her eyes hardens.

"I saw you leave for work one morning as I was coming back home myself," he adds quickly.

They are walking beside the park now. The little boy is running and sliding towards the fountain.

"What kind of work do you do then?" she asks politely.

"I work in a hospital."

She nods.

They've turned into Henri-Julien and are a couple of doors away from her apartment.

"Right here," she points towards her black iron gate.

"I'll bring them to your door," he offers and she opens the gate, arriving before him at her door.

"Thank you," she says now, and waits for him to put the bags down and depart before she takes out her keys.

He waves goodbye and crosses the street with a light step, heading towards his own door.

ℯ

She walks into her hallway with some difficulty, trying to squeeze all the bags through the entrance at once before she can take off her boots and enter her apartment. She quickly glances at her son, whose nose is running in two thin lines toward his red lips. He is standing there, bundled up in the thick winter jacket, immobile, lest the clear liquid from his nose enter his mouth. She kicks off her boots and runs to the bathroom in search of tissue, returning a moment later with folded toilet paper to wipe the boy's nose. The door slams shut, and across the street John is once again left standing at his window to stare at the yellow rectangle through a veil of hovering snow.

He has to prepare for work, he realizes, the laundry having taken more time than anticipated. As he showers and dresses, he thinks about the woman, wonders where she lived before moving here a year ago, whether she's a widow, a divorcee, a single mother, and how to find out. Memories of her small feet enveloped by pointy ankle boots are interrupted by the thought of the old cursing man leaning on his walker at the hospital in his slow advance towards the washroom. A sinking feeling overcomes John as he leaves his apartment to take the bus to work. He walks, chin to chest, against the wind, which pushes him back and sprinkes him with stinging snow dust.

e͜

"Life in Montreal is not for the faint of heart," says Anne as she takes off her padded winter parka, her face red and moist. "It is for bears," she adds, bending down to take off her boots.

"Anything new?" she asks John.

He shrugs before bending down from his chair to tie his shoelaces. An emergency light blinks. "The old man," he says, "I'll go see," and rushes down the bright corridor.

The old man cannot breathe, twitching this way and that, gasping for air. John gives him oxygen, calls for the doctor. "Call my wife," the old man hisses between gasps, "call her, tell her I'm going."

Anne has walked in meanwhile and is going over the chart for the wife's telephone number.

"We're looking into it, Mr Fournier, and the doctor is on his way," she leans over to tell him calmly.

Meanwhile the oxygen mask has had its effect and the old man is somewhat calmer.

Before leaving the room, Anne again scans the chart.

"There is no next of kin here," she whispers to John.

e͜

Half an hour later the old man is sleeping, his life prolonged a little longer by the tall, blond Dr DeVries, whose instructions spilled out of his thin pale lips like phrases in a telegram. John is sitting once again at the front desk, in the light of the only lamp lit at this hour, while the ward is asleep, and a couple of nurses walk up and down silently. He is not writing tonight. He has not even bothered to take out his pen, preferring to daydream instead. His neighbour's black ankle boots on his mind remind him of the single white slipper on the sidewalk, far away. A dull ache returns inevitably to his centre, that place between chest and diaphragm, and does not easily dissipate. Years have passed, more than a decade, he muses, and still I crumble at the thought.

℮

There is never a beginning to these things. One moment there is the shadow of an eyelash, velvety glances, a shy smile behind which laughter hides. That moment permeates everything past and present; the autumnal crispness, the smell of coal smoke spewed out by chimneys, bald, pruned mulberry trees lining the avenue, an old, one-storey bungalow sitting innocently between tall apartment buildings, like a rich and somewhat senile aunt invited for tea by her large covetous nephews. It carries with it daylight and sunset, the half-eaten meal left on the plate, the doorbell, the night air bearing drunkard's singing from the invisible distance. It is all of life at once, in an ever-present moment.

℮

She was Selma, named after Selma Lagerlöf, the Swedish author of her mother's homeland. There were yearly trips to Stockholm, duvet covers on her bed with pillows made of goose feathers before anyone had ever heard of such things. He slept on their softness, her perfume in his nostrils, next to a bookcase filled with unintelligible books she had read entirely. There was one snapshot with a small, cheerful, cotton-haired lady, her grandma, and another of her on a swing in grandma's farmhouse some- where near Stockholm. Her mouth was open, her eyes shut, her teeth peeking out, tiny and orderly from behind happy lips. She wore narrow soft denim shoes with white laces, her hair in a boy cut gleaming like a copper pot on her head. She was a teenager in that photo.

℮

The red light goes on, then a buzz, startling John. He sees Anne rushing down the corridor. The old man is having another crisis. Dr DeVries is called once more. A while later, Anne comes back with a baffled expression.

"He wants his wife. What do we do?"

"I guess we tell him he doesn't have one," replies John. "Is he calmer now?"

"Yes."

He walks down the corridor and enters the old man's room. It smells of medication and iodine.

"Mr Fournier," John speaks close to his ear, "I've come to keep you company. Is that all right? Just blink for yes, and do nothing for no." The old man blinks and opens his eyes to look at him.

"Are you feeling a little better now?"

He blinks again and looks at the ceiling.

"I miss your cursing very much," John says and pats the old man's hand gently. It feels cold. "I hope you're in shape to curse again in the morning."

The old man tries to smile.

"We're trying to find your wife for you . . . is she in Montreal?"

There is no movement from the old man.

"You see, when you checked in, they were supposed to make you complete that paper, but they probably forgot . . . "

The man keeps staring at the ceiling.

John continues, "I thought I could find it in the phone book. You're sure she's not in Montreal?"

The old man remains immobile.

John sighs.

"Any kids?"

The old man does not answer.

"Is your wife anywhere in Canada?"

No reaction.

"You're going to have to help me a little if you want me to find her."

The old man turns his head. There's bewilderment in his eyes. John hears a deep sigh and then the raspy voice says faintly, "I . . . don't . . . know where . . . she is."

John nods and pats the man's thin arm gently. "Don't worry."

He looks out the window at the city lights flickering like candles in the distance, wondering what to do next. He leans closer to the man's ear. "If you give me her name, I can do a search for you."

"Later," says the raspy voice and he closes his eyes.

"Good, I'll let you sleep, then. Hope I find you cursing tomorrow night."

The old man does not react, he seems to be asleep. John stands up and walks quietly away.

He finds Anne at the desk looking through patients' charts.

"And?" she asks curiously.

"Nothing . . . " He doesn't want to talk about it. He wonders if the old man will make it through the night, or if, when he comes to work next, he will find the room empty.

The rest of the night is uneventful, except for the usual changing of sheets, and walkabouts and time spent eating his mortadella sandwich, yogurt, and cereal bar. He thinks of Selma, and the old man living his last days on earth without any sign of the woman he called his wife. He cannot help but wonder if he too will become a cursing old man, dissatisfied with his lot, bitter as his days become scarce like the air that enters his lungs. He tries to imagine the circumstances of Romeo Fournier before he came to the hospital to die. His life decades and decades ago. He sits down and reluctantly takes his green notebook out. He begins to write the words Mr Fournier might whisper to him tomorrow.

℮

"My wife was married to someone else when I met her. In those days, divorce was not an option for most people, certainly not for us Catholics, as you can imagine. Not that she would have chosen it; who am I kidding? She worked in a diner across the street from my shop, as a waitress. Her husband was a factory worker. They had come from Rimouski to settle here in Montreal soon after they got married. I was a

cobbler, by trade . . . hmm . . . My shop was on Mansfield, below de Maisonneuve.
You wouldn't remember; they've torn the whole block down. The first day I saw her
she wore black ankle boots, a red coat, and a small black hat with a feather on the
side, she had blond curls all around the hat, black leather gloves. It was snowing very
hard that day; two feet on the ground and more was coming. She was struggling to
walk on the sidewalk. Her first day of work, that was. I saw her from the corner of
my eye, through the window, this red stain on white snow, beautiful coils the colour of
a wheat field swinging around her head. I dropped whatever I was doing, and . . .
Funny, I still remember what I was working on; it was a pair of brown men's shoes,
the soles needed fixing, size 12. I dropped the shoe and went to the door, which had
a glass window, and stood there watching this girl trying not to get her feet wet in the
snow. Her cheeks were red from the cold. Just as she was reaching the diner, she
slipped and fell. I ran out in my slippers to help her. I grabbed her hand and pulled
her up. Her handbag had fallen down, I gathered the stuff that had fallen on the
snow, put everything back in the purse and gave it to her as she rose. All I saw were
the blue eyes and red cheeks. 'Merci,' she said, brushing the snow off her coat and
avoiding my eyes. She was so shy . . . I opened the door to the diner and let her in,
she smiled and nodded before I returned to my shop in my wet slippers and soaked
feet. I couldn't work for the rest of the day. I kept staring at the diner door. It was
February 4, 1948. Sometimes I'm not sure of the year I was born, but that date
I always remember.

"*Every day I waited for her arrival and every day I went for coffee at least three*
times to be able to see her, and then I stood by my shop window to watch her leave at
the end of the day. This went on for months. I hadn't the courage to speak with her
or tell her my feelings. When I saw her wedding band the first time she served me
coffee, I was devastated. I knew it was a dead end for me, but couldn't help myself. I
resolved never to go to the diner again and forced myself not to look out the window
when she arrived. It was the longest day of my life. I didn't want to eat, didn't want
to work. I just sat there, feeling miserable, among my old shoes. I hoped she'd get fired
or get a job elsewhere, so I would be forced to forget about her, you know. But destiny
had different plans for me. To this day I don't know why on earth my mother called
me Romeo when there were so many other names, Pierre, Maurice, Joseph . . . I used
to think if I had such a name, she wouldn't have been already married when I met

her. Well, let me tell you, Romeo is not a pretty name to be stuck with when you get to my age and you're all alone."

Here he took one long breath that made his chest wheeze and stopped for a while to rest. His breath was hollow when he spoke.

"I better hurry in the telling, or I'll die before I finish it. Her name was Jeanette. A perfectly good name to raise a family and lead an uneventful life, actually. But that didn't work out either. So perhaps names cannot be blamed for destiny after all . . . I don't know." He rested some more, wheezing and coughing.

"One day she walked into my shop. She had a pair of shoes that needed new soles. I kept her there for a little while, making small talk. She was comfortable enough to tell me about her hometown, her family and friends and how she missed her life there. She was happily married, I believe, in those days . . . A year or so later, something happened to change her life entirely. Her husband's arm got stuck in machinery, and he lost it. It was his right arm. He could no longer work and she could hardly feed them both with her waitressing job. So I hired her husband to help me out with the orders, put the shoes on the shelves, the kind of stuff a left-armed man could do. Yeah, that's right . . . Not that I needed the help or could even afford it. I had to move from my apartment to a rooming house on St-Urbain just so I could pay this guy a salary. I really don't know what got into me. I should have simply ignored the whole thing, she would have taken her husband and returned to where she came from and that would have been the end of it. I might have fallen in love with another girl, married, had children, right? But no, an evil little voice in my head convinced me it was a perfect plan; I could enter her life this way, be her protector, and if not her love I could at least bask in her gratitude. Selfish, conceited bastard. I wanted all the crumbs if I couldn't have the bread . . . The poor devil, her husband, was trying so hard to please with his single arm that it was painful to watch day after day.

"I used to sit on the fire escape of my rooming house on hot summer nights. It was a filthy old building. Once in a while a raccoon would pass by, looking for garbage down below. I used to sit there and have a smoke. Sometimes I wept in the dark night. I was a young man, and I thought I deserved better than loving another's wife. When you're young, you think like that. You deserve a better childhood, a better love, better chances, more money. It's all about deserving and feeling sorry for yourself. Then life happens and you realize you don't deserve what you get, you only deserve what

you make. Am I wrong? Anyway, it's too late to tell me, if I am."

The old man tried to smile at this point of his story, a small bitter smile, and as he did, a coughing fit overtook him and wouldn't let go of his thin ribcage. After a lot of wheezing and trying to shake the mucus out of his congested lungs, he continued.

"See? I'm still a conceited asshole trying to fool you into thinking I've grown wise. I can tell you're seeing through me. Those dark brown eyes . . . I've been bitter all my life and I have arrived at my last five minutes of truth just now, with you as my witness here. What is your name?"

John stirred a little in his seat as if coming out of a trance. *"John."*

"John. Hmm . . . What was I saying, John?"

"That I'm your witness."

"Hmm. Perhaps you'll write my story someday. I always thought someone should . . . So, as I was sitting there weeping, one hot night in July, a thought came into my head, like a nail driven through my skull . . . I realized I wanted her husband dead. I did. I had him in my shop all day, every day, and I wanted him gone. Are you shuddering?"

"It feels a bit draughty here by the window," replied John as he moved away.

"It looked like repulsion for my person," continued old Romeo staring at him. *"Don't tell me you've never had such thoughts yourself, not even a fleeting one?"*

John remained silent, as the man continued his story.

"He was a good man, her husband; he was kind. I was guilt-ridden to even have such a fantasy, to be so evil as to wish her unhappiness. But that was my only chance to win her affection, first as a caring friend, a shoulder to cry on, and perhaps, in time, as a lover. I would make her love me."

He looked at John and shook his head. *"You work in this hospital, cleaning people, shaving them, moving them, you see them day after day, these old, rotten wrecks washed ashore with no hopes of ever being mended. This ruin here, named Romeo, who curses as he creaks, whose pee stutters as it trickles, this here . . . "* he waved his hand vaguely towards his immobile legs, *"was once a vigorous man who enjoyed a good steak, who skated on ice like any pro, yes . . . Hard to believe, eh? This old ruin,"* he continued soberly, *"had a heart that raged against its cage."*

John couldn't help himself asking, *"What happened to her husband? Did you . . . ?"*

The old man turned his head towards him. "First, you tell me something . . . Why do you do this work?"

Taken aback, John mumbled, "I need a job to pay my rent, like everyone else . . . "

"Hmmm. Perhaps I was mistaken about you . . . "

He turned away and closed his eyes signalling the end of the conversation. John leaned back in his seat, puzzled. Why did the old man want to hear his story all of a sudden?

"What is it you want to know?"

"Whether you're worthy of hearing the rest. It is, after all, my life I'm telling you about. I need someone worthy, not any old jackass who's wiping butts for rent money."

"I am running away from my life." John said, growing pale in the darkened room.

"How so?" The old man's eyes shone. Between two blinks it almost seemed like he had grown more youthful.

"There was a woman, difficult circumstances, I was young . . . I had to leave, and here I am." John stopped as if he had already said too much. His heart started thudding in his ears. The old man nodded.

"I knew you had something you wanted left alone."

"I'm all right. So, what happened, will you tell me or am I still a jackass?" John smiled as he said this.

"You're still a jackass to think you can run away from anything; but that's okay." The old man took a deep breath and began once again to tell his story.

"I never committed the crime. Not in the legal sense. No weapons, no struggle, nothing that would put a man in jail, no. What happened was worse . . . "

He closed his eyes and it looked as though he were falling asleep. John wondered whether he should wake him or leave the room, when the man reopened his eyes and said, "I got my wish." He sighed.

"I went to work the next day, opened the shop, sat on my stool, started fixing a broken heel while eyeing the street. I looked forward to his coming because she accompanied him into the store, helped him out of his coat, kissed him goodbye, stroked the back of his head and smiled at me kindly, promising to bring us coffee from the shop. You know, it was a very loving, tender moment and it moved me to see her affection, even though it was for the wrong guy. I was sickeningly jealous of that love,

yet I couldn't help but admire it at the same time. The man had everything in his favour, I thought. He was much more handsome than I was; even through the distortions of my envious eye I could see this. The only thing I had in my favour was my second arm, really. Well, my only other advantage was my mood, which generally was more upbeat than his. You could see the man was making huge efforts to conceal his misery. His eyes were always sad and defeated, even when his lips smiled. The ghost of his arm pursued him wherever he went. He would go to scratch his right hand with his left hand. His fingers would just hang in the air for a moment and he would look around to see if I noticed. There were moments, in the middle of some movement, when he seemed to hesitate. I used to wonder why he hesitated like that. Then it dawned on me. He expected his right arm to do something, and it wasn't there to do it. It always took a moment of hesitation, and then his body would move differently, having recollected the absence of his lost limb. He once told me she wanted a baby, but he couldn't even imagine that, although he felt he owed it to her in a way. He wouldn't be able to hold the child, or even play with him and so he changed the conversation whenever she brought it up. I was grateful for that, of course. I did not want to imagine him dead, with his child between us to remind me forever of his absence. With my luck, the child would look exactly like him, anyway."

The old man sighed and closed his eyes again.

John wished Romeo Fournier would tell his story faster, without so many halts and meanderings, lest he die before telling him how it all ended. He touched the man's cold, bony hand after a long silence and reached over to ask, "Do you want to sleep a little?" hoping he would say no. Romeo Fournier opened his eyes, looking disoriented. "Was I sleeping? What happened?"

"You were telling me about her husband not wanting a child and you wanting him dead," he whispered in the man's left ear. As he moved away, he caught a whiff of talcum powder and disinfectant from the man's wrinkled neck. Outside the window, the flickering lights of the city beyond the dark forest were getting dimmer. The darkest time of the night had passed, promising Romeo Fournier another day. As if sensing his thoughts, the old man gazed into his eyes for a while. His greying irises looked liquefied, shining in the dim night light coming from the bedside.

"Do you . . . have to . . . leave?" he whispered.

"Not yet. Not for another couple of hours, unless they call me. It's a quiet night."

The old man nodded. "Where was I?"

"You wanted him dead and got your wish," said John, hoping Romeo would stick to a linear account.

"How awful that sounds, coming from your lips," he said. "I should have asked for a priest, instead."

"I could get you one if you like."

"I want you to know . . . there is more to Romeo Fournier than this line you just threw me."

"I imagine," John nodded, feeling ashamed.

"If you're going to write my life story, I hope you'll put in more than that, jackass," he scolded feebly, before continuing. "You'll have to put in all my dreams and desires, not only the ones that will send me to hell."

John nodded again.

"Give me some water," Romeo ordered, frowning.

John got up to pour water into the glass from the ochre plastic jug. There were still some remnants of ice cubes floating on the surface like jellyfish. He walked over to the old man, cranking up the head of the bed. He then put one arm around his back and with the other he slowly trickled the water into his parched mouth, making sure it did not spill down his chin. The old man nodded when he'd had enough and John placed him back carefully, and wiped his mouth with a paper tissue.

"One day you will be where I am; dying in some smelly hospital room," Romeo said after resting a little. "You remember that, when you write my story. Don't you scribble some dimwitted trash, you hear?"

"Okay," said John feebly.

"I loved that woman, do you even know what that means?" He tried to take a deep breath before continuing, "I ruined my life for her and she never found out a thing." He began coughing again. It sounded like a howl.

John hoped the man's anger would dissipate as he recalled the only woman he ever loved. He ceased struggling with his cough and was out of breath for a while. Colour had risen to his cheeks, giving him an almost healthy glow.

"It just occurred to me," he said, "that all my belongings in my room at the home will be thrown away once I'm gone. There is a photograph of her. It was taken at a picnic. She was sitting next to her husband on the grass. I tore him out. It's one of

those black and white pictures, with zigzags all around the edges. I took the picture at the Mountain, a few weeks before he died. I wish I hadn't torn him out, now . . . But anyway, it'll all be garbage soon. She wore a short-sleeved white blouse and a flowery skirt, spread open like an umbrella around her waist. She had her feet tucked underneath . . . I used to spend a lot of time with them, on weekends . . . I was discreet, you know, always hovering on the edges, a solicitous friend, more his than hers. But I think the husband knew why I was there. Once in a while, when he thought I wasn't looking, he stole harsh glances my way. He needed me and hated me at the same time. She was oblivious. At least, she acted that way; she must have known, though. Women know these things before we do, don't they? I can't blame her; she needed support and she used me. As long as she pretended not to know, it was acceptable. Morally, I mean. To her . . . And I knew this. I knew if I ever declared myself, I would give her no alternative but to take her husband and leave. The three of us had this tacit understanding of why we were all there."

John could see the old man was forcing himself to speak evenly, using all the energy he could muster.

"Would you like me to freshen your forehead with a washcloth?" he asked.

"Yeah, okay . . . " Romeo closed his eyes while John went to the sink to wet a washcloth in lukewarm water.

"Here, how is that?" John asked, placing the carefully folded washcloth on the man's creased forehead.

"Good," Romeo said, then broke into a sob.

John froze, not knowing what to do in the face of such an outburst. Finally he leaned close to the old man and tapped his shoulder. Then he held the man's hand in his. He felt sheepish.

"I'm sorry," Romeo said, "I feel so lost. Damn!"

"Want me to go ask for the priest?"

"Not yet."

John continued to gently rub Romeo's limp arm. He pulled a tissue from the box with his other hand and dabbed the man's tears.

"Where were we?"

"You had a tacit understanding, all three of you."

"It seemed that way. I used to wonder if by that same understanding she suppressed *her feelings for me. I read so much into every single gesture and smile . . . I would go to my room and cogitate about how she said something to me, and what she might have meant by that, beneath the appearances . . . It may seem silly to you now in the telling, that a grown man would fall so hard for a woman from afar. Everyone seems so practical nowadays. When they do autopsies on your generation, they will find the heart intact. It is the dick that now suffers all the injury and pain, having replaced the heart in action. Wouldn't you say?"*

John burst into laughter.

The old man nodded, now suddenly animated. *"Laugh, laugh . . . You know it's true."*

He became thoughtful, then smiled a little. *"Whereas, yours truly here, with a name like Romeo, was guaranteed to under-use his dick and overuse his heart."*

John shook his head, still laughing. *"You're quite a comic too, aren't you?"*

"A lie-down comic," quipped the raspy voice. *"Give me some of that water again."*

John filled another glass and helped Romeo drink. Outside, the snowfall had resumed, filling the square window with white.

"Almost daybreak," sighed John, sad to think he would soon leave the old man alone.

"I'll wait for you, don't worry," the old man said, looking better than he had during his entire stay at the hospital.

John told him so.

"Eh . . . I have something to look forward to, I guess. How long have we got?"

"About an hour more."

"I feel okay. Do you want to hear the rest?"

"Sure."

"That day, I sat on my stool, worked, looked out the window and kept checking my watch. They were late. I thought something had happened to the train tracks. It always did in winter. Half an hour passed. Then one hour, two more . . . I knew something was not right. Before lunch I got a phone call. It was her voice, coming into my ear from what seemed an unearthly distance. Faint, almost erased . . . It still chills me to remember.

"'Romeo . . .'

"'Jeanette, c'est toi?'

"'Romeo . . .' a deep sigh, muffled sobs . . . 'Romeo,' she kept repeating as if trying to gain courage. 'I'm at the hospital.'

"'What happened?' I asked.

"'Roger,' she whispered, 'il est . . . m . . . mort.' There was an avalanche of sobs. 'Il est m . . . m . . .' and she couldn't say it the second time."

e

For years afterwards, she kept going over that fateful moment, recounting it. When she awoke that morning, he'd got up before her and made her coffee while she showered. In all their years of marriage he'd never made her coffee, until that morning. In the doorway, her back to the wall he kissed her before they left the house. It was like their first kiss; warm, tender and heart-wrenching. She was swept away. They walked to the train station hand in hand. Nothing was said. Once in a while he put his one arm around her waist and pulled her close. It was such a change from the moodiness he had had since the accident, she said. She felt hope for the first time in a long time that morning as they walked to the station. They paid their tokens and descended the stairs to the platform. The train would come in three minutes. He turned to her, struck by a sudden realization and said: "Could you run up and get me the paper. I forgot to get it. Be a darling and go, you'll do it much faster than I could. We still have three minutes." "What about the token?" she asked. "Don't worry; I have an extra one, here." He shoved his hand into his coat pocket and handed her the token. She ran up the stairs, breathless. There were a couple of people before her waiting to pay for their newspapers, one of whom was a lady who couldn't find the exact change in her purse. Finally, the lady found her change. The man who was before her didn't take much time. She paid for her paper quickly, ran to the turnstile, stuck her token in. She heard the grumble of the train entering the station. Agitated, she ran down the stairs and saw, at that same moment, a crowd gathered at one end of the platform looking at the tracks. The train had stopped part way into the station. There was panic. "Call an ambulance!" someone shouted. An official started telling people to move back and up the stairs. She knew.

e

Romeo's eyes were closed. John saw a tear trickling sideways under a closed eyelid down to the pillow.

"That's all," he whispered. "I took care of her as well as I could. I never dared ask her to marry me. I hovered around the edges of her life, aware of her wishes before she could formulate them, always present when she looked up. I created coincidences; running into her on the street when she felt lonely, meeting her on the train to work. Don't ask me how I did it. I don't know where I found the strength . . . But so it was. Then, one day she left. I don't know where. She just vanished. Like a dream. I searched everywhere. I tried to find her family. Nothing. She did not leave me a note even. You know you're in deep trouble when you travel across the ocean on some vacation you don't even want to take, and pray to run into her in the streets of Lisbon, or wherever. I have ached for her, for the mere sight of her walking in the snow, for the last forty-five years." His chin trembled as he said this and tears ran down his cheekbones, pooling into his ears. "I still wonder if she sensed my thoughts. That I wished her husband dead the night before he died. Why else would she leave like that?"

Romeo closed his eyes. He had spoken for most of the night and now the sun was rising in the middle of his window, filling the edges of his room with slivers of orange light.

"Your time's up, jackass. Go home." Romeo strained as he uttered this, in a sudden change of mood.

John rose from the chair beside the bed, stretching his arms and legs. There was a quick crackling of bones and cartilage as he bent his knees, reaching close to the man's ear to whisper, "I'll see you tonight, old man. Do you want some water before I leave?"

Romeo lay immobile, already fast asleep.

❧

John looks up from his notebook at Anne putting on her boots, getting ready to go home.

"I've never seen you so engrossed in your Thoughts-of-the-Day. You've been sitting there frowning and writing away for the last three hours."

"Did I miss anything?" he asks. "Is the old man okay?"

"Sleeping," she reassures him. "Looks like he'll be around a while longer. Are you staying here for the day shift too?"

"Huh? No, I'm getting out now." He stuffs his notebook into his packsack and hastens for the elevator.

Outside, he inhales the humid winter air, steps onto a thick, crunchy carpet of snow. Snow-clearing trucks make their way uphill. Traffic is hesitant, moving up and down the avenue, on a layer of slush. The street smells of exhaust and snow. A car passes too close to the sidewalk, splashes his pants. His bus arrives; he boards it, leaving white and brown tracks down the aisle as he goes to sit down behind the old Asian lady with the faded dragon bag on her lap. Gazing out the window aimlessly, he is tempted to take out his notebook and read the story of Romeo Fournier. He resists the urge, still feels raw inside.

The Asian lady did not get off at her usual stop, the corner of St Lawrence, he realizes as he pulls the chord. The bus slows down and stops. He gets off and sees the lady watching him from the moving bus. He crosses Pine Avenue and walks down Henri-Julien to his door. He turns around to peek at the yellow door across the street. The few stairs going down to her outside door are covered in a mountain of snow. He imagines the expression of dismay on her face when she opens the door. He goes into his apartment, grabs his shovel, crosses the street, and clears her entrance and stairs before returning to clean his own. Sweating profusely, he finally goes into his apartment, yanking off his toque. He stands there, his back against the door, trying to steady his breathing. Then he takes off his boots and goes to the small window. The yellow door does not open when he expects it. He waits a while longer, feeling his eyelids drop with fatigue. He goes to his bed, leaving his pants on the floor.

℮⁓

As he is drifting off to sleep in his darkened apartment, the woman across the street leaves her house with her son, crossing paths with Leonard of the Great Danes in the park a minute later, while Romeo Fournier dies in his hospital bed, having struggled for one final breath.

John once again falls into his dream of the fisherman leaving the shore, his sun-bleached hair caked up into rigid curls from the salt. This time, John is Romeo Fournier. He knows he is dreaming, and wonders who this fisherman is whom he cannot see. He wants to fly over the boat to get a glimpse of that face. In dreams, he reasons, you can do that. But his legs are leaden and won't move. He remains glued helplessly behind the fisherman pulling the oars, taking him out to the open sea. What is he going to do with me, he wonders, once we are far from everything? Throw me overboard? "Hey you!" he shouts, "where are you taking me?" His voice comes out shakier than intended, adding to his worry that the mysterious fisherman will now know his level of anxiety. The fisherman keeps pulling the oars. John taps his brown shoulder. "Tell me where we're going!" he commands. No response. The fisherman goes faster. "Take me back to the shore, right away!" John shouts furiously though he is very scared. This is a lousy dream, he rages, and opens his eyes to his darkened room on Henri-Julien Street. "What's with this blasted fisherman?" He blurts this out loud instead of using his inside voice. "Why can't I have a decent sleep for a change?" He continues muttering until he falls asleep again.

When he awakens late that afternoon, he once again goes to stand and wait behind the blinds. The street lies under a haze. He has slept through the considerably loud noise of children leaving school a couple of hours earlier. The woman appears from around the corner, walking alone towards her house. He grabs his coat and shovel to go out, to be doing something when she arrives. He is shovelling his entrance as she approaches him quietly and taps his shoulder. "Thank you for shovelling my entrance this morning. It was very nice of you. I don't mind doing it myself, though. It's good exercise . . . " She smiles, lifting her shoulders and dropping them. "Thanks anyway," she says and goes away as he croaks something that sounds like, "You're welcome." He would like to speak more, but she has already sauntered off in her tiny black boots and is gone. Discouraged by his failed attempt to engage her in conversation, he walks to a café on St-Denis Street for his usual double espresso. Surrounded by wood and coffee smells, he salutes the saxophone player, who is warming his fingers between his gigs on the street, and the poet born in Argentina (the one with the beautiful pen) who publishes articles in the *Cosmo* under a feminine pseudonym. They are having a heated discussion on chauvinism in Quebec and the many ways in which it has hampered their once promising careers. It seems to John, who half-listens to their conversation as he sips his coffee, that they are having the same debate they've had over and over, on a daily basis, seeking refuge in the warm bustling café from the poverty of their circumstances in the dark, wintry Montreal afternoons. The little bells on the door chime, announcing each newcomer, who brings along a gust of frigid street air. John feels the blood rush to his face when he sees the woman arrive with a tall lanky fellow with black curly hair and a moustache. As they study the blackboard behind the counter for their choices of coffee, the dark man's arm slips around her waist. John bends down to pick up his packsack, from which he laboriously retrieves his pen and green notebook. He feels he can neither leave nor stay without being noticed. They have ordered their cappuccinos and turn around to find a table. She squints as she looks around, and as her gaze lands on John she smiles briefly with a nod. She finds a place farther away, which she points out to the tall man. As they walk towards the designated spot, he lets go of her waist and holds her arm. Her face is momentarily lost as she pulls off her scarf, hat, and coat in quick rough gestures. The tall man, looking elegant in a Spanish type of way, removes his black wool coat. He slides down the wooden bench with the ease of a panther to sit next to her. John observes her rosy face, glowing and fresh. He supposes they made love before coming, from the way she forms an unfocused, lusty smile. They sit very close, the tall man and the lovely neighbour, their arms entwined, as they sip their cappuccinos; he, whispering things in her ear and she, lifting her chin up and exposing her throat as she laughs, eyes half closed. All John can think of, as he sits there trying to look occupied with his notebook, is that she is taken. He is devastated about a woman he doesn't even know, he reasons to him-

tied to his toe that corresponds to his name on some list. He lies frozen and naked, waiting for the residence he called home before the hospital to make arrangements for his incineration. Amato, the keeper of the Fridge, nervously lets John in to see the corpse, wondering why he, who generally wheels the dead to his door and no farther is suddenly curious to visit one already inside a drawer. John explains that they had become friends, and he felt the need to pay his respects one last time. As he leaves the Fridge he quickly and secretly shuffles through Amato's records and takes mental note of the name of the residence where the old man used to live.

℮

The next day, instead of taking Bus 144 home, he decides to pay a visit to the residence on René Lévesque. He remembers the days a couple of decades ago when the avenue was called Dorchester and was lined with creepy rooming houses and low-rise apartment buildings. He used to live in one of those houses which no longer exist, having given way to a skyscraper. There were cockroaches the size of a thumb and human misery he was unprepared to find in the world-famous city known for its European flair, sophistication, bilingualism, et cetera. He found the rooming house on Dorchester, not far from Concordia University and Guy Street. On de Maisonneuve St West was the statue of Norman Bethune in a little triangle with a dried-up lawn across from Guy metro station. He remembers standing there among pigeons to admire the monument of this Canadian hero, a doctor, on his first day.

He had made a friend soon after his arrival in Montreal, a guy from India named Vish, who also lived in the rooming house and showed him how to use the washer and dryer in the basement. Vish explained he was a communist and had worked in a bank in Bombay, and saved all the money he could to come and do his masters in economics at Concordia. He spoke a sophisticated British English, John thought, and waved his left hand in small wrist flourishes while tilting his head from side to side as he spoke. He had never met a man from India before, and was excited to have already befriended someone from such a great distance after only a few hours in Montreal. Vish was living on a very tight budget; the cover on his bed was an old yellow electric blanket less the wiring, apparently discarded by someone else and never cleaned. The Indian, whose poverty of circumstance was in direct contradiction to his generosity, offered to cook supper for him. He heated oil in a black and much corroded wok, threw in spices and seeds that made a crackling sound as they burst, before adding onions to the mix. John's first supper consisted of spicy stir-fried onions on clumped white rice, which he was taught to eat with his fingers, sitting on the floor with crossed legs. Vish, who had been in Montreal a couple of months longer, became his guide around the city, taking him to a bank, then to his appointment at the Immigration Office, and to the local police station for fingerprinting. But John could only stand to live in that rooming house on Dorchester for three months.

He nods to himself as the memories of another life come flooding in. He looks up to find the building where Romeo Fournier used to live; a refurbished old brick cube for this government-subsidized seniors' home. He speaks French with the man at the reception. Monsieur Lajoie refuses to release any of the old man's belongings without proper authorization from him; but Romeo Fournier, argues John passionately, is unable to sign anything, being already quite dead. The absurd discussion goes on for a while, during which John discovers that there is no next of kin, and therefore what is not to be released to anyone without proper authorization will go to a garbage bin, also without proper authorization.

"Proper authorization from dead people is a big thing around here," mocks John in English having given up arguing with the stubborn receptionist who is now even more on the defensive on account of the English spoken in his presence, without proper authorization. John reverts back to French and asks if he could please have one look around the man's room, to pay his respects as it were, having been his only friend and acquaintance at the end of his life. Monsieur Lajoie agrees reluctantly and takes him upstairs where he unlocks the door to Romeo's room.

The ochre curtains are drawn, and in that penumbra John sees a bed that was slept in, with the covers pulled back and the sheets crumpled. There is a lampshade on the night table. The only photo in the small rectangular room is in a frame on a circular table beside the window. He advances towards the window and pulls the curtains, peeking over his shoulders at Monsieur Lajoie, who gazes around with a bored expression. He looks at the photo, and he sees her. A woman in her early twenties with wheat blond curly hair sitting on the grass with her flowery skirt open around her tucked-in legs like a fallen parachute. She is wearing a short-sleeved white blouse and is smiling at the camera, while her body leans to the left a little, as though in an attempt to get closer to someone just outside the edges of the frame. It is a black-and-white picture, the borders cut off in a slightly crooked way.

"May I at least take this photograph?" asks John, placing his hands on the table to steady himself. Meanwhile the room is turning around him, furniture occasionally appearing to go upside down. He reaches into his pocket for his folded handkerchief to wipe his face.

"It is a little stuffy in here," he whispers.

"Are you okay?" asks Lajoie.

"Not really. I need to get out of here, or I'll faint. Can I take the picture?" he repeats.

Monsieur Lajoie glances quickly at the picture without much interest and shrugs his shoulders.

"Just remove it from the frame."

After wiping his forehead with a quick gesture, John puts his handkerchief back in his pocket and quickly takes the photo from the frame.

"Merci, Monsieur," he nods slightly, sticking the photo into his breast pocket.

Monsieur Lajoie mumbles "Bienvenue," then nods sideways towards the hall, indicating to John that he has already spent too much time attending to him.

Once in the metro, John hesitantly takes out the photo from his pocket. His heart starts thudding. The woman gazes at him in her flowery skirt and blond curls. He turns the picture over. A tidy feminine hand-writing in faded ink says "et Jeanette Daoust." Right behind where the husband was torn from the picture would have been his name, "Roger."

John, unaware of his surroundings, shakes his head from side to side, mumbling, "How could such a thing happen?" He hides his face inside his palms for the rest of the ride.

$\backsim$

He goes to the café hoping to meet Pablo, the Argentinian poet. Lack of sleep and his emotional upheaval have combine into a headache squeezing the inside of his forehead. He pushes the café door, to be greeted by the comforting aroma of coffee and the soft sounds of a sax-ophone. The poet in his thick brown turtleneck sweater and black cor-duroy pants is sitting by the window reading the papers. The rubbers he generally wears over his shoes are on the floor at the side of his table, lying one on top of the other in amorphous softness. His black shoes are impeccably shined, despite the snow and salt of the sidewalks.

"Pablo!"

The poet turns his bespectacled face slowly towards the door, his auburn beard gleaming in the light.

"Hmm?"

He lookes at John, senses something is not right from the wide open eyes and moist face.

"Pablo, good you're here! I need to talk to you," John says and sits across the poet without waiting for an invitation, and leans over.

"You're a poet, you would know about these things."

"Don't get your hopes up, my friend," Pablo rolls his eyes, "out there, I'm Serena Brown, the *Cosmo* writer. I just wrote an article about calories and how to count them. I know all about calories. Trans fats, too . . . "

"Not joking. This is a serious matter, Pablo. I'm going nuts."

"I'm all ears."

"There was this old man . . . " John tells him the story of Romeo Fournier in the hospital, then the story of Romeo Fournier in his green book, and how he found the picture of the woman Romeo described in his green book in Romeo's room. He takes out the picture from his pocket and shows it to him.

"Even the name corresponds. I thought I made it up, Pablo, but it's real. How do you explain such a thing?"

Pablo stares at the picture for a while. Then he looks up.

"You don't."

"That's it?"

"What else? Leave it alone. Are you able to explain everything else?"

"You think you invented something, and it's been there all along."

Pablo bursts into laughter. "My innocent friend, that happens to me every single day. You write a sentence or a phrase about an idea that descended upon you—because they always do, don't they; descend, I mean. Well, maybe they ascend . . . hmmm, I'll think about that later—and you think it's the most original thing you've ever thought up. Meanwhile, someone else said it better a century before you, or even a couple of thousands of years ago . . . You'll get over it."

"You don't understand. You're talking about words. I'm talking about real people with names, pictures. Strangers that I didn't know existed. And I wrote about their lives."

"Writing is dangerous business, John," Pablo says and leans across the table as if sharing a secret. "If you can't handle it, quit scribbling with that cheap pen in that green book of yours." He then straightens his newspaper to announce the end of the conversation.

"That's great!" exclaims John, visibly upset, gesticulating. "You can dismiss me with a line like this and continue reading your paper, 'Writing is dangerous business, John' . . . , he imitates the poet, shaking his torso side to side. "Pablo, has this ever happened to *you*? And no, I'm not talking about how someone wrote a better poem. No offense, pal, but that is entirely conceivable to me. What just happened isn't!"

"Calm down, hombre, everyone's looking at you," Pablo tells him in a softer voice.

John looks around and a few faces turn away.

Pablo continues with a smile, "Moments like this, I just know you're Mediterranean, even though you've never said a word about your origins."

"Don't change the subject, I need to *know*."

"Listen, man. This has never happened to me, okay? And it is fascinating. But I have no trouble with it. Because . . . ," he takes a deep breath, puts down the paper on the table and thrusts his hands up in the air, "is there order to all this? If so, are we capable of ever fully comprehending it? Once in a while, lightning flashes, and a poor soul gets a glimpse of something. Today, you're that poor sod, John. That is all I have to say on this. Can I read my paper now?" He picks it up and straightens it once again.

"You know what, Pablo?"

"What?" The Argentinian asks, not looking up from his article.

"You're a pompous ass."

Without waiting for the reaction, John gets up and leaves the café.

⁓

At home, he leans the picture of Jeannette Daoust against the small jade statue of Buddha smiling among the papers on his desk. He sits and stares at the picture for a long time. Feeling sleep overcome his eyelids, he removes his socks and lies down on his bed, fully clothed. Tomorrow, he thinks, I will go to the library. Then he begins to dream fitful dreams from which he wakes up a couple of hours later and gets ready to go to work. He boards the bus, feeling feverish and weak. He leans his head on the window pane, feeling his guts wiggle as the bus advances and slows in the evening traffic. I need to start exercising, he thinks, or this engine is too old. He gets off in front of the hospital, looks up at the lit windows, thinking of the invisible corridors and elevators inside carrying the moribund, the dead, the ones to be operated, or giving birth. He imagines the huge vats of discarded organs, growths, and limbs. The pills that go in the mouth, hundreds of toilets flushed simultaneously sending excrement and illness into the St Lawrence River a few kilometres away. A castle on top of a city, the inside of it shaped in neat cubes, housing so many moans, so much despair and hope. Doctors with clean fingernails walk back and forth wearing white gowns; nurses efface themselves behind their uniforms and squeaky white shoes. A clean cube within a castle in the middle of the city, on top of a hill, overlooking a wide frozen river. My universe, he thinks, as he walks through the automatic doors, greeted by the diluted, soured, coffee smell wafting to his nose from the cafeteria. The elevator grinds to a halt; he enters, standing next to quiet strangers jaundiced by the neon lights.

Anne greets him with, "You're married with four children, I hear. Room 415 told me. Shame on you! After ten years of working with me and keeping mum, you go tell Room 415 your life story . . . "

"Forget about it," John says, annoyed. "She invented the whole thing, and I didn't dispute it. That's all. I'm not married, I have no children. And now this is our own little secret. Room 415 likes the story; so don't disappoint her, okay?"

"You're too weird. I don't even know your age after all these years!"

"What do you need it for?"

"Everybody knows everybody's age."

"I don't care about anybody's age. Are you collecting statistics? What exactly?"

He removes his boots and takes his uniform out of his packsack.

"I don't know . . . I don't even know where you come from!"

"And you need to know, because you'll visit my village on your next holiday?"

"Relax, man, will you? You know where I'm from. It doesn't take anything away from me, does it?"

"No. But I never asked you. For me, it's like asking to see my passport. Then, you'll be scrutinizing for a darker shade of skin, listening to my accent, watching for any signs of riding camels or milking goats. Next thing you know, you'll be saying, 'You people'. Screw it, Anne. This famous Canadian mosaic-thing . . . You got it for free. I earned it. And that is all you need to know, okay?" He shakes his fist, which holds the bunched-up uniform, and goes towards the back to get dressed. As he walks away he mumbles something she cannot hear. He stops in his tracks for a moment, then continues, disappearing behind an automatic door, leaving Anne frozen in her posture.

When he returns, dressed in pale green scrubs, Anne is sitting at the desk, looking busy with forms and a pen.

She doesn't look up when he comes to stand by her. "I'm sorry, Anne. I didn't mean to snap at you."

He knows she's wounded when she lifts her face from her paperwork, her glasses poised on the tip of her nose. "Okay," she says simply and continues to write.

"New glasses?" he asks.

"What the hell's wrong with you?" She puts the pen down.

"I haven't slept in two days."

"Take a snooze. Not much going on right now. I'll wake you up."

He nods and walks through the automatic doors to the staff room, where he lies down on the olive-green vinyl sofa, curling up with his back to the door. He hears footsteps going up and down the corridor, a woman's garbled voice falling off a distant microphone at regular intervals, the occasional giggle, bits of conversation mixed with shuffles and footsteps that lull him to sleep.

e∽

As the garbled woman's voice on the speaker calls a Dr Papageorgiou three times, John's neighbour from across the street sits on her bed in her bedroom at the far end of the apartment and bursts into sobs. Her long chestnut hair has cascaded to the front of her face, which remains hidden behind her hands as her body shakes. The boy, who is already in bed and about to sleep, opens his eyes, hearing her muffled sobs. He squeezes his stuffed dolphin toy closer to his chest and waits.

Twelve doors up, Leonard of the Great Danes is leaving his house with the two dogs, lighting up his cigarette as he walks down the stairs to the sidewalk. He takes a deep breath of smoke and releases it as the animals pull him forward, their leashes tightening. He half runs across the street, the dogs ahead of him. As he passes in front of the woman's house, he tries to look through the window, which is dark, a faint glow coming from the back of the apartment. One of his Great Danes defecates a soft and runny pile as they walk on towards the park. Leonard curses between his teeth as he sees the steaming brownish puddle in front of her iron gate. While his animals pull him across the park, his jogging girlfriend is turning the corner from St Lawrence to Marianne, sweating in her jogging suit and woollen toque. The Spaniard who has just gotten off the subway at the west end of the city has turned the key to his apartment door and enters it in the darkness, reaching for the light switch. He looks at the coats hanging in the closet by the door, then down at the rubber mat. He tiptoes around the apartment quickly, checking the bedroom, the kitchen, the bathroom.

Then he sits by the black telephone and reaches over to dial.

Across the city, John's beautiful neighbour is brushing her teeth in her pyjamas, checking her swollen eyes in the small bathroom mirror. She plans to put a compress of teabags on her eyelids to take away the puffiness for work tomorrow as she spits the foam and rinses. Next door, the child has fallen asleep squeezing his dolphin. His fingers slowly release their grip on the toy and it tumbles onto the covers. The telephone rings. She rushes for it and picks it up before it rings again.

Her voice comes out breathless. She listens and responds softly, "Haven't I told you not to call me at this hour? I don't want him to wake up."

She listens some more, nodding impatiently.

"Well, there's nothing else to . . . "

She listens briefly and changes her tone to interrupt, "It's up to you. I'm done waiting. Please don't call any more." She hangs up and walks back to the bathroom, where she puts on her night cream and turns off the light.

The phone rings one more time. She lifts the receiver and puts it down, then removes the plug from the jack.

૯ᐟ

She lies down, the softness of the pillow enveloping her head, and sighs a long plaintive sigh before letting herself go to sleep. As she falls into a deep dream, a few kilometres away John is woken up by Anne. He sits up on the vinyl couch, disoriented for a few moments, and rises to go back to his post. At the west end of the city, the Spaniard is still sitting on the armchair by the phone when his wife enters the house. She sways a little as she removes her pumps and waves to him vaguely, then rushes down the corridor to the washroom, unable to keep a steady course. He does not move. His eyes return to the phone. It is ten PM. He slowly rises, puts his coat on, and leaves the house while his wife is still in the bathroom. He walks to his car in the crisp night air, sits down, hands on the cold steering wheel. The interior smells of processed alcohol, her breath. He rolls down the window slightly and, turning on the engine, drives east under the dark skies, watching the illuminated windows on the way, some with curtains drawn, others wide open. He can catch, from the corner of his eye, a lampshade here, a ceiling fan there, as the windows speed by, then he comes to the restaurants and the people sitting inside, and couples walking in the streets, their breaths puffing out small shapeless clouds. At the corner of a small intersection he spots a dépanneur. He stops the car, walks in, looks at all the flowers and pays for a bunch of fresh-looking yellow mums and daisies.

They look pedestrian, he reflects, but at least they're cheerful and it's late at night. He throws the bouquet on the seat next to his and continues driving until he gets to Henri-Julien. He sits in his car, looking at the yellow door for a long time, before he picks up the bouquet and walks towards her house. His foot sinks into the soft brown mound left behind by the Great Dane outside the door. "Mierda!" he exclaims and hurls the bouquet towards the door, rushing back to the street, dragging his soiled shoe on the ground to get the sticky brown excrement off his sole.

There are brown footsteps leading to the door and away down the sidewalk the next day when John returns from his night shift. Hurried brown steps, up and down the few stairs and around the now slightly hardened old mound. His curiosity leads him to the bouquet of half-frozen flowers lying awkwardly beside the entrance. Must have been thrown, he thinks and smiles, imagining the scene. When he goes to his house, instead of rushing to bed he stands by the window, waiting for the yellow door to open.

A few minutes pass, before the door is pulled in, remaining ajar for a while. The boy is looking for his shoes; the snow is gone. John sees him kneeling down to tie his laces. The woman appears dressed in her coat, holding the boots. She kneels beside her son and talks to him. He shakes his head and points outside. She goes to the door to look at the sky. She sees the brown steps, the disturbed mound, and the bouquet at the side of her entrance. She bends daintily to pick up the flowers, checking the wrapping for brown stains. Satisfied that it's clean, she smiles, looks at the mums, and disappears into the dark apartment. She returns to take the boy by the hand and steps out. John opens his door at that moment, pretending to go to the corner store. She sees him eyeing the mess in front of her apartment.

"Someone left me this, and flowers," she says and nods, pointing vaguely at them.

"Do you know who the secret admirer is?" he asks, smiling.

She raises then drops her shoulders quickly. "It's not you, is it?"

"I wish I had thought of that first; but I'm afraid not . . . maybe Leonard? His dog left you the brownie, and Leonard, the daisy?"

A torrent of laughter cascades out of her small frame.

"Maybe . . . Lucky me, I got two presents!" She waves and walks away with her boy.

"My name is John, by the way," he offers.

She turns towards him and smiles.

℮

She created laughter, he sighs, gazing at her disappearing figure, and *now she's walking away with it*. He wants to follow her, find out where she works, who she is, as he closes his apartment door once again and enters the dark, quiet, musty space. It happens to him sometimes, before falling asleep, to feel removed from the lump of his body lying in bed, floating higher and higher into the air, beyond the ceiling, beyond the roofs of houses and the tar-encrusted gravelly tops of tall buildings, watching tiny cars and trucks speed back and forth on grey highways like ants rushing to and fro, and then higher, where the air feels cold and rare, where he struggles to breathe as he watches the occasional eagle or owl hover with its magnificent wings spread open, gliding, with a slow graceful flap and then another, subtly changing direction in the vast empty skies that belong to it and to which it belongs. Up there, away from his own kind, his insignificant life and clumsy body, his being, fills with yearning for another existence, unavailable to man. And precisely at that moment comes the rapid fall from the empty skies to his cramped and darkened room where his grotesque limbs lie patiently awaiting his return.

"Who is I?" he wonders uneasily, suddenly feeling the *I* as a current passing through his body without the pompous ownership of a conjugated "*am.*" And yet, I am the one wondering about it. There is someone who owns this body, which is I, and there is that to which this body belongs, which is also I, he marvels uneasily, wondering if he has understood himself at all in the space which has suddenly grown vast in his mind.

The picture of Jeanette Daoust, he notices before falling asleep, is still leaning against the small jade statue of Buddha that was given to him years ago. She is smiling from a distance. He feels a shudder move through his chest as he watches her. Who knows where and who she is, he thinks, and yet here she is, smiling in my life now, from half a century ago. Is there a picture of me in someone else's life? Someone in Sweden for instance, whose name is perhaps Arvid Lundsgard. He closes his eyes and Selma appears with her red head and agile limbs, her features well defined and settled, time having creased the skin around her eyes somewhat, her forehead crossed by a line that will become a fold in a few decades. She is dressed in a beige suit; her neck covered in a light blue silk scarf, an expensive wedding band her only jewelry. Her look is that of studied elegance, that of a rich man's wife who can have everything she wants yet chooses austere minimalism. There is something sad about such visual restraint; her hair that once spoke of glorious sunsets is now straightened and pulled into a tight bun. Nothing glistens. She walks around inspecting her grandmother's farmhouse which has become hers. Outside, a breeze is swaying the empty swing this way and that. It has just rained, and the sky remains overcast, not having emptied itself completely. The smell of wet earth has seeped into the house somehow, despite the closed windows. A chauffeur sits in a limo waiting for her to complete her inspection. Otherwise Selma is alone. She walks up the stairs to the bedrooms. Her door is wide open, next to her grandmother's. She hesitates in front of her grandmother's room, her eyes blurring with the pain of her absence. She enters her room in which is a bookcase with the two stuffed dolls made for her by her grandma, some books of adolescent adventure, a couple by Agatha Christie, brownish pages of *Little Women*. From the window, which is framed with white curtains, she sees a blur of green, brown, and grey; trees still covered in mist, the soft wetness of fields wrapped around them.

She pulls out the drawer of her desk, her hand reaching for the box within, which she now removes and opens. She expertly reaches for the bottom of the pile of photographs in the box and pulls out a black and white rather grainy picture of John. He is in his early twenties, his hair covering his ears in long black shiny strands and parted on the side. A turtleneck sweater peeks from under the leather jacket, his elbows lean on the railing of a ferry boat. He has turned his head sideways to smile for the camera. His smile says, "Remember this." And she does. She remembers the cold moistness of his palm that crisp fall day when she held his hand after putting the camera away, and the cry of seagulls covering the steady hum of the boat's engine. From a corner of her eye she saw the water being parted by the ferry, turning over foaming, never leaving an empty space, enveloping the boat as it forced its way through the soft, transparent thickness. They stood there quietly, eyes fixed on the other shore, palm to palm. It seemed there would be no end to this moment. It would continue into the distant future, obliterating the daily necessities that applied to everyone else's life: the brushing of teeth, the consent of others. It seemed the future and the past had converged here, on this boat crossing a bay, carrying this fluttering of spirit, this moist clasping of soft palms, this youthful desire to be nowhere and everywhere at once.

Then he had simply said, "I got my papers. I'm leaving in a few weeks."

She had known about this; that he was going through the immigration process for Canada, that papers had gone back and forth, that he had gone for X-rays, blood tests, and finally, a stool test for which she had provided the sample in a rectangular matchbox. There were details such as these that made them laugh. But now there was a plane ticket. So he was leaving her. Not exactly, he corrected, since he had asked her to go with him. It has been a complicated story in her mind, for many years, until now when she looks at the black and white "Remember this" picture which had lain blind, flat, and untouched in her hidden box for years.

She remembers the jolt somewhere in her guts when she heard the departure words. The ferry was still cutting through water, the water was still returning to the ferry asking for more, the seagulls kept squawking with their careless beaks and small bald eyes. A blue plastic bag floated farther away, gathering brown hairy seaweed around it. She let go of his palm. The other shore arrived, and they got off. On the pier, she stood facing him and said, "I prefer not to see you any more. I'm going now. Goodbye."

He did not let go of her. Instead, came the longest night of her life, with its blind stars shining between parted curtains, darkness suffocating their light, and the crushed, hurting thing between them which they could not bear to throw away. The night that almost cost her everything.

We threw ourselves away instead, she reflects, sitting demurely at her dresser, with her trapped, aching hair roots and bland elegance. *At least I did.* She puts the picture on top of the pile and takes the box under her arm, ready to leave the farmhouse. As she walks down the staircase, her heel gets stuck between wood planks and she stumbles, grasping onto the railing to steady herself. The box has flown out of her grasp, contents flying in every direction; pictures, mostly, some rocks and small memorabilia scattering all around the landing and the living room floor. She collects whatever she can and hurriedly leaves the house, getting back into her limo, box in hand. She fails to notice that John's picture is not among the things she collected until she reaches her hotel room in Stockholm. In a couple of hours, her plane leaves for Athens, where she now resides with her two children and her husband, an executive in the tobacco industry. Her heart sinks as she sits in the hotel room, on the freshly made bed whose flowery beige cover smells of nothing special, looking through the contents of her box, not finding the picture she most wanted to keep. There is not enough time to go back and look for it now. She calls Inga, her grandmother's friend and helper in her late years, who cleans and tidies the empty farmhouse regularly as it sits uninhabited, waiting for Selma to make a decision. She tells her there may be photographs and small objects here and there under the furniture in the living room. She stumbled, dropped a box; the contents sort of flew out. She is fine, yes. Just some souvenirs she cannot find that mean a lot. If she finds them to please mail them to her in Athens. Doesn't know when she will return; probably in a few months. Thank you, she says, thank you, and hangs up.

e⌃

Inga Lundsgard gets up the next morning and takes her youngest child, five-year-old Arvid, with her to the farmhouse. He likes the swing outside and running in the muddy meadows with his rubber boots. The skies are still overcast, fine drops of rain come down delicately to flatten themselves on the windows of her townhouse. She drives her old car to the farm, listening to Vivaldi on the radio, Arvid sitting in the back, gazing at the passing scenery absentmindedly, lulled by the gentle sounds of a violin mixed with the monotonous swish of the windshield wipers and the sight of thin rain misting up the dense forests. He does not yet realize that he will forever associate that particular piece of Vivaldi's with peaceful rainy days and the fruity smell of his mother's blond hair filling the car. His eyes close and he soon falls asleep. Inga sees his closed eyes from the rear-view mirror, the pink cheeks, the lowered head and half-open lips, the palms loosely open so she can touch their softness with her gaze. He opens his eyes when the car stops. The boy rushes out drowsily to find the swing he remembers in the garden. He hurriedly sits on the wet swing and starts pushing himself back and forth with great seriousness. A couple of minutes later he is running in circles, his tongue stuck out to gather raindrops. Finally he is in the house asking for a drink. As his mother takes out the thermos from a basket to prepare his hot milk, he has squeezed himself under the couch where he finds a photograph lying face down. He turns it over to find the black and white face of a man, not a very interesting discovery; nevertheless, it is a treasure and he stuffs it in his coat pocket.

Inga finds nothing under the furniture. A couple of hours later she puts Arvid in the car and they return to town listening to Vivaldi from where they left off, with the rhythmic swishing of wipers and raindrops running down the car windows in small streams. Arvid once again falls asleep trying to keep track of all the rivulets of water racing across the window pane, wondering why they run sideways.

When they reach home, Inga removes the boy's raincoat and hangs it in the bathroom to dry. Meanwhile the forgotten photograph remains in the pocket, its edges curling up from humidity while Inga makes a collect call to Athens. There is no one to take the call and after a while she gives up trying.

⁊

Selma, meanwhile, is attending a cocktail party in a tony neighbourhood of Athens, holding a champagne glass with polite indifference, listening to an older tobacco man's monotonous drone. Her husband is across the room talking with animation to some fresh-faced colleagues and a secretary in high heels wearing clothes too expensive for her budget. They laugh at everything he says, their faces set into smiling masks of deference between the jokes. As she nods absentmindedly to the old tobacco man's comment, it occurs to her that her husband may be sleeping with this high-heeled assistant. There is a hint in her rigid smile, thinks Selma, of having heard all these jokes before, in more comfortable quarters. She imagines her husband's hairy, naked backside as he writhes and pushes down on the secretary in a hotel room; her legs flying around, breasts in his face, her vacant smile waiting for him to finish so she can go home, watch TV, and eat popcorn as she wonders why her life feels so drab at night. She despises the expensive clothes he buys for her which she has to wear when she meets him in hotels, yet squeals in apparent delight whenever a box appears on her desk. She continues to watch TV and eat popcorn with her hair in her face and her legs hanging from the sofa's arm. This is what Selma sees as the woman puts her weight on one high-heeled foot, then the other, trying to remain elegant in her made-up face. Since her trip to John's photograph in her grandma's house in Sweden, something has changed in this cocktail scene, Selma realizes. The thought of her husband's hairy backside makes her want to chuckle as the old tobacco man asks her a question to which she has to find a quick reply. She is not entirely sure what the question was, although she did hear the words, and now they are piecing themselves together in her mind while she lingers a little longer in the hotel room watching the unsuspecting lovers flap their awkward limbs here and there in passionless acrobatics. Her husband unexpectedly turns and smiles at her from across the room. She knows he will soon cross the floor to come near her, put his arm around her waist to guide her away from the tobacco man towards another conversation.

"Are you bored?" he whispers now.

She nods.

"Go home?"

She nods again, smiling.

He takes her out into the cool evening and they drive away.

She looks at him sideways in the car as he sits in his dark expensive suit and cologne, focused on the road, quiet. Fifteen years of marriage versus a grainy black and white picture. Architecture versus hut. She wonders where John lives in Canada, whether he still lives at all and if so, whether he still . . . Whether he still . . .

And if he did, then what? Her husband changes gears and puts his hand lightly on her knee. She looks at him gazing at her. Maybe he isn't sleeping with the secretary after all. He stops the car on top of a hill overlooking the city and the starry night.

"Where are we?" she asks, straining to see.

"Not home."

There's a question in her eyes.

"Why go home?" He asks. "The kids are away, what's the big rush? I've never taken you here before . . . "

"But you have been?"

He looks away for a moment, and then back at her. "Yes, I have been. What do you think?"

"Okay," she says and looks around vaguely.

"Some days after work I come here and sit in the dark. Thought I'd show it to you."

She nods.

"Are you unhappy?" he blurts out suddenly.

"Is this a we've-got-to-talk kind of thing?"

"I don't know, is it?"

"If you've got something to say, just say it."

"I work all the time. I'm . . . "

She remains silent as he searches for words.

" . . . here now. I thought, you know, we could have a genuine moment, just the two of us."

Behind the car, from farther up the road come strains of *bouzouki*, laughter, and the roar of confused voices in a heated conversation. She feels lonely sitting in the car with him. Two strangers in Athens. Two strangers anywhere. Very unlike him to make such efforts for an earnest conversation, she muses, absentmindedly playing with the soft corner of her silk shawl.

He tries again, "Years ago, when you married me, was it for love?"

"Of course," she replies.

"I was away a lot, even then. The first year, I used to see you hiding tears, leaving the room suddenly. I never asked you, but I want to know the truth now. Why were you crying?"

She winces a bit, he catches it.

"I felt lonely."

"On account of my absence, or someone else's?"

The question fills the car with silence. She remains speechless for a while, baffled.

"I don't understand this line of questioning. Have you been unhappy? Is that what we're talking about?"

"Maybe . . . Look, I see my life, my accomplishments. Beautiful wife, good kids, money, job, everything we have put together, you know, and I don't feel anything. I don't feel . . . There's no room in all this for me, you see, and I wonder if it has been like that for you, if we sort of got trapped in this together. What did it all mean?"

"Do you like what you're doing? Your job, I mean. The tobacco thing . . . " She finds something else for him to focus on.

"I guess; the deals, the adrenaline. Why?"

"Manufacturing something that kills people . . . "

"Oh I see," his gaze hardens. "I have been offending your conscience all these years while you sadly went shopping for your Vuitton bags or whatever. Please!"

"I didn't say that. I just thought perhaps . . . Well, perhaps you now feel you could have done better with your life."

His eyes narrow. "Could you have done better?"

"I honestly don't know."

"Was there someone else?"

"I won't answer that. And you probably don't want to have to answer it either. Can we go home now? I'm tired."

He turns on the ignition in a brusque gesture and backs away from the scenic spot. They drive down the hill, through empty highways, back home. She goes to the bathroom to wash her face; he turns on the TV and sits down, pulling his tie this way and that, to loosen its grip while he stares blankly at the screen, which keeps flashing meaningless images. His eye catches a corner of white satin fabric, he looks up and there she is, in a nightgown, her face pale without the make up and her copper hair loose around her shoulders in waves.

"Why did you marry me?" she wants to know urgently. Just as he is about to open his mouth to answer, she cuts in, "Because of my hair?" she pulls the hair to a side, "because of my figure? My education? Because I would look nice at your boring cocktail parties?" She is working herself up to an angry glow.

He turns off the TV. "If I said yes, would you admit you married me for status?"

"You're so harsh with me! I wanted a real marriage, something good. I worked hard for it, I think. Two kids. Following you around while you chased 'adrenaline, deals'. How dare you say I married you for a designer bag, or some such thing? How about that secretary who was making eyes at you tonight? Do you want to answer that question?"

"Why are you so angry at me?"

She stands there, frozen in her fury. He has a way of diffusing her so she can never quite burst out in anger. She slumps next to him on the couch, her leg touching his.

"I'm not," she sighs. "Look, I don't know what you're getting at with all this, I'm tired, so let me just ask you this . . . "

He nods, but she doesn't see it. Her eyes are focused on the floor, for courage, mostly.

"Are you asking me all these questions because you want a divorce? Is this what you're truly asking me?"

He breathes and holds it in before releasing it slowly. "Not really . . .

I think I was asking you to notice me, to love me again. I don't even know that you ever did. I don't know anything any more. You're like this distant visitor in my life. You're never quite there; you're never quite mine . . . Yes, you had my kids, you followed me around wherever I went, you never complained and had the most exemplary demeanour all these years. Sort of like an illusion. I mean, where have you been? Do you understand? I hope you have at least been somewhere else, because you haven't been with me!"

She puts her palms together in front of her and dangles them off her knees.

"I didn't think you actually needed me there. Did you? You needed my appearance. But you don't need anybody. I wonder if you even miss the children when they're not there. You hardly notice them. Seriously, you have the nerve to tell me I wasn't really there?"

"See, I tell you you've been intangible, you tell me I've been absent. That's fifteen years of . . . not much there."

"So, why do you beat around the bush and give me this 'I want to be loved by you again' when you actually want to end it? Why be hypocritical about this? Fifteen years of not much there is not worth saving, in the first place. What is there to save? No, thanks. I'd rather save myself from these cocktail parties where I have to watch you flirt idiotically with assistants that make you feel superior while I'm stuck listening to some suit who bores me to death. I'll take the kids and move to Sweden. I have my grandmother's house. I'll be fine. You make the arrangements for our divorce."

As she utters these words, the smell of waxed wooden floors from her grandma's distant farmhouse inexplicably comes to her nostrils, making her want to smile and weep at once. *I'm coming back home, grandma.* She wants to say this out loud to her grandmother who is no longer there to hear it. She knows she has finally unravelled the mystery of her own life, wanting to weep for the old woman whose love has now come to set her free.

Her husband sits motionless; his tie dangling sideways, the limp remnant of a life lived in constraint. He had expected a rather different conclusion: one of consensus to save the thing, to reach into depths and extract meaning through shared suffering. A kind of heroic excavation project to be undertaken together that would ignite a flame. Not this simple, sleek statement of rejection. He has difficulty understanding how the conversation got to this point. Worse, he has difficulty imagining his life going forward. He is the picture of pathos, Selma observes, feeling sad. *I failed to rescue him.*

e⟩

Arvid Lundsgard is sleeping though this exchange in a slightly different time zone while rain continues to empty the sky of clouds, pattering on dark windows through the entire night. Across the Atlantic Ocean, down the St Lawrence River on the island of Montreal it is late in the afternoon, and John is about to awaken from his sleep. He hears the freezing rain beating upon the windowpane and the chaotic merriness of children's voices as they walk and slip down Henri-Julien. His eyes open just before the alarm clock rings. He reaches over to press it down, continuing to lie in bed with eyes open. The dream he is unable to clearly remember has left him exalted and drained. He suspects Selma was in it, and there is the vague memory of a boy named Arvid something, whose connection to John's life is no longer clear. Rising slowly, he throws off his covers and rushes to the thermostat to raise the heat in his damp apartment.

Standing immobile under a hot shower he is still under the effect of the dream that has failed to reappear in his memory. Hot steaming water hits his body, entering his mouth and nostrils, the scent of wet soap filling the air. He wants to take a day off from work, go to the café, write something in his notebook. As the water continues to run over his face, he feels cheerful, thinking of the phone call to the hospital telling Anne he is not coming to work, hanging up. Perhaps he will run into the woman of the yellow door as he leaves his house. There may be opportunities to converse. He whistles as he lathers his face for a shave. The entire evening belongs to him. He might even be able to sleep at night, like he used to before this job.

As he leaves the apartment, the yellow door remains closed. He crosses Carré St-Louis carefully, sidestepping sheets of ice covering the park. The trees are gleaming in the pale afternoon sun, their branches and trunks trapped in ice, like immense glass ornaments rising out of hardened snow. He feels an irresistible urge to walk off the path, force his boots into the icy mounds, crunching into them, leaving gashes and cracks on the delicate whiteness. He stops and turns around, and through a cloud of breath watches his footsteps, harsh and angular on the ice. The fading light touches the broken ice, scattering small slivers of purple shadow all around, each footstep like a miniature glacier beneath a sunset. A handful of disturbed ice, he muses, has the magnificence of vast, unseen landscapes in the world. He remembers the book of Canadian landscapes he used to flip through as a child, the pictures of white icebergs, the immense lakes tucked among mountain ranges; all those pictures that made him want to be an explorer of the vast silences of the world.

He crosses St-Denis and enters the café and hears strains of gypsy music. The bearded poet is sitting at his usual table by the window with a familiar-looking man John can only see from the back. Pablo waves at John to join them. He orders his coffee and goes to Pablo's table. When he comes face to face with his beautiful neighbour's lover, he hesitates, suddenly not wanting to sit down. Unable to find an excuse, he pulls up a chair. The neighbour's lover is Salvador. Pablo explains that his sullen countenance is the result of a heart problem.

"Are you ill?" asks John, concerned.

"No, hombre!" Pablo replies, "problems of the heart, impossible love, heartbreak . . . like this!" He knocks his fist over his chest a little too energetically before rubbing it.

"Ah," John nods politely, feigning ignorance to hide his curiosity. There is silence around the table as Pablo taps his finger on the surface.

"Perhaps I should leave you two to your discussion. I'll go read the paper," John says and rises.

"No, no, sit," Pablo insists, not even looking at Salvador, who remains pensive.

"Have you two known each other a long time?" John inquires, not quite knowing what to say.

"About two hours or so—although I've seen him here a few times before, with a beautiful woman." Pablo turns to Salvador. "You'll forgive me, but back then I was looking at the woman, mostly." He rolls his eyes to show his appreciation. He continues, looking at John, with a smile, "She's the problem. I want that problem . . . "

Salvador throws Pablo an outraged look, and Pablo hastens to add, "I meant to say, love is a good problem to have, you know, if one were to categorize problems. But not yours, of course, Salvador; yours is not a good one. Certainly not."

John looks at one man, then the other, wondering what they could have possibly discussed in the last two hours. His café au lait arrives steaming in a bowl.

"So," he says to Salvador politely, "may I ask what kind of problem, or is it too personal?"

Salvador looks into John's eyes and says, "Imagine being married to a woman you have loved at one time, but whose illness has destroyed everything, all your dreams and hers too, and you cannot leave her because you worry. Meanwhile, life beckons in the shape of a gorgeous woman and you are madly in love, but she will not have you, because you're married."

Pablo is looking out the window absentmindedly, having already heard the story.

John takes a sip from his café au lait.

"You are torn between duty and love," concludes Salvador, shaking his angular face sadly.

"Does your wife have parents?" asks John somewhat furtively, not wanting to overstep the boundaries of good manners.

"Her entire family have disappeared; mother, then father, then, a year ago, her only brother."

"Good God! Where have they gone?"

"He means they're dead," Pablo explains.

John takes another sip of his coffee, thinking of the frozen flowers and dog shit in front of the neighbour's house. He would like to find out more about her, some mention of her name perhaps.

"I'm sorry," he says, curious to know what kind of illness Salvador's wife suffers from, but is unable to ask. "I hope your wife gets better, and maybe you can work things out with her, instead."

"If she can get better, then I can leave her," Salvador says. "I don't love her any more."

Pablo sighs. "Love is the only feeling I know that can be heavy and weightless at the same time. It can crush you flat or lift you up. Like an elevator. You know, if you're wise, you take it to the ninth floor and park it there. Use the stairs if you need to."

John sips his coffee quietly.

"What are you talking about?" Salvador turns to Pablo angrily. "Are you making fun of my situation?"

"No, no . . . Not at all. I'm just trying to bring some levity to this afternoon chat. Obviously, neither John nor I can solve your problem. So what is there to do? I mean, you either stay with your wife and help her, or you leave her and help yourself. In either case, only one person benefits.

"Question is, can you truly help someone when you feel you're their prisoner? And, if you leave your wife, perhaps it will change things in her life for the better. Whatever you do in the end has to express your conscience and beliefs. I don't know . . . I mean, let's say your wife is in a wheelchair. You don't stop loving her because of this. You don't accuse her of destroying your dreams—at least I would hope not . . . If you're accusing your wife of destroying your dreams and hers too, that means that her illness has a moral dimension, right? You know, you feel she has a choice. She chooses to be sick and make your life miserable. Or perhaps you choose to see it in that light because it justifies the absence of your affection for her. In my opinion, Salvador, and you won't like what I'm about to say and I hope this won't end our two-hour friendship immediately . . ."

Salvador taps the tabletop impatiently. "Just say it will you? Why do you keep stretching things so much?"

"Fine. When you married her, you promised to love her in sickness and health. Right?"

"Yes, but I didn't know she had this . . . thing, then!"

"Regardless, you then found out she did. You loved her then, didn't you? So, years passed and she continued to remain sick. Then you got tempted by a beautiful woman. You thought, I have a right to this happiness, too. Why not? It was a cowardly thing to do. On the one hand, you have the sick one at home, and on the other, you have this other one who deserves better than what you are able to give her. So your desire for happiness overtook your conscience. You messed things up. But instead of saying so, you say you're torn between love and duty. And in your own eyes you're already a bit of a sad hero."

John starts coughing, having aspired coffee into his trachea. Salvador rushes to get him a glass of water while Pablo gets up and pats his back.

"I'm okay," John manages in between his fits, his cheeks having turned red, "please sit down, I'm going to be fine."

Salvador sits down, looking at his hands stretched out on the table in front of him, trembling slightly.

"In other words, I broke my promise in a cowardly way," he says gravely.

Pablo remains silent.

"On the other hand, did my wife not mislead me when she did not tell me of her illness?"

"Did your wife know she was ill?"

"I think at this point," Salvador says, "the problem is practical. Even if I've been guilty of a moment of cowardice, or weakness, and frankly I prefer to call it inspiration myself, the fact remains that I have either to stay with my wife in a loveless marriage or leave her and find love."

John interjects, "Why not ask your wife? I mean, maybe she doesn't love you either."

Salvador looks up at John with a bitter smile. "I have to wait until she's sober first, and that could take months."

John gazes out the window, realizing he will not get much information about his neighbour this afternoon. He feels sad thinking of the tall, lithe Spaniard sitting next to him whom he first saw in an elusive moment of happiness beside her in this very same café, considering him the luckiest of men, envy burning his guts. Some people, he muses, can live with unhappiness for a very long time. Others cannot bear it. The tolerance for unhappiness, is it a virtue? Or is not being able to bear it the true virtue? What is the measure of true virtue? John has forgotten all about Pablo and Salvador, his cold café au lait in the white porcelain bowl that now looks grey in the vanishing light, the evening darkness descending stealthily upon the busy street. He does not hear the words being said around him, the laughter, the strong smell of marijuana on someone's winter jacket as he walks into the place. He is caught up in his silent pursuit of elusive answers, here, in the midst of a bustling evening on St-Denis Street.

Pablo taps on the table and awakens him from his reverie.

"I'm hungry," he says. "We can go to my place and have spaghetti de los pobres. I have some red wine, something perfectly aged to give you a headache and take away all your illusions about quality. I also have Aspirin for later."

Salvador emits a small pained laugh and accepts. The three men step out into the cold air to join the bustling crowd. John remembers he needs his gloves. "I live over there," he points, "it will only be a minute." They walk towards the square with its solitary fountain and its bald tree branches, still icy under the yellow auras of the lamp posts. As they enter Henri-Julien, Salvador exclaims, "You live on the same street as she!"

"As who?" John asks, feigning ignorance and hoping to get her name.

"As one of my good friends," replies Salvador, not wanting to divulge. John unlocks the door and invites the men inside while he goes searching for his gloves. They stay on the rubber mat in the entrance so as not to take off their boots. As he rummages through the cloth sack containing scarves, toques, and single gloves, from the corner of his eye he sees them observing his place. The two men are quietly looking around, each in his own way, eyes stopping on small objects, paintings, bedcover, and bookcase. He notices, in their curious gazes wandering through his apartment, the pleasure of having suddenly discovered someone else's intimate space.

"Do you want to have a shot of cognac before moving on?" he asks.

The two men look at each other in agreement and proceed to take off their boots. As they wander hesitantly into the small apartment, John turns on all the lights and goes for the cognac bottle under the sink.

"I have tequila or wine glasses. What do you prefer?"

"Wine glasses," suggests Pablo, his eyes on the black and white picture leaning on the small jade Buddha statue.

"Is this the picture you were telling me about the other day?" he asks.

John pretends not to have heard as he pours cognac into the wine glasses and hands them to the two men. "To your health," he says, lifting his glass, and takes a sip that burns as it goes down his throat.

Pablo sits on the couch and sighs. "Looking at us, one can presume that we are all lonely men in our middle years, congregating. Slightly pathetic, isn't it?"

John retorts, "I'd take out lonely and pathetic. Can we not congregate as men without being pathetic?"

"Oh, but you know what I mean! We have Don Juan here who's got wife and lover—well, ex-lover—and is sitting with us instead. We have an aging, unpublished poet who writes crap for *Cosmo* under a woman's pseudonym, who could never to this ripe age commit to anything more serious than a passing affair, and John, the mysterious, who works when the world sleeps, and sleeps when the world works, and therefore meets no one but the sick and the dying."

Salvador lifts his glass. "Let's enjoy this uncomplicated moment, then, while it lasts."

He takes a big gulp, showing his teeth while swallowing, and rises from his chair to go to the window.

"Interesting view you've got from this window," he says, watching the yellow door across the street.

"It is the only window worth looking out from in the entire apartment. The others face brick walls, a messy backyard. Have you noticed that here in Montreal duplexes and triplexes usually have windows in the front and back? Never on the sides. There is usually a long corridor and rooms in the middle that don't receive any natural light."

"Rooms within rooms . . . ," adds Pablo.

Salvador moves away from the window with apparent dismay and goes to sit down beside Pablo on the brown, somewhat deflated sofa.

"Do you know anything about your neighbours?" Salvador asks. "This area looks like the sort of place where you'd know your neighbours."

"I know some of them," John says, and proceeds to tell them about Leonard of the Great Danes and Margaret the Hungarian spinster next door who was born in the very house in which she is now getting old. He adds that there is a single mother with a small boy who moved in not too long ago, right across from him, but he doesn't know their names. He glances at Salvador, who nods, without saying anything. "Then," he continues, "there is Marcel, the French Canadian filmmaker, and a Brazilian musician further up. The Brazilian always has a party going, and once in a while, I go. Her name is Carina. She is single, as far as I know, so Pablo I can introduce her to you sometime so you can stop congregating with a bunch of pathetic middle-aged men."

Salvador rises from the couch once again and goes to the window to look out.

"You really must like the view!" Pablo exclaims, "or you're awfully restless."

Salvador finishes his cognac in one gulp. "Shall we go for that famous spaghetti of yours?" he asks, glancing at his watch and out the window once again.

"Are you expected somewhere?" asks John. "You seem to be checking your watch a lot . . . "

"Hmm . . . Yes, actually, I need to leave soon. Can I take a rain check for the spaghetti party? I really would like to spend the evening with you two, but I just remembered something I have to do. I'm so sorry about that!"

He looks flustered as he goes for his jacket and boots, still apologizing. Within minutes, he is ready to leave and opens the street door.

℮

Salvador inhales the dry, cold winter air, feeling tiny icicles form in his nose as he closes the door behind him. He stands outside, immobile, his eyes fixed on the yellow door.

John has motioned to Pablo quietly to come to the window. The two men hide behind the blind, watching Salvador pause on the sidewalk, the cold wind blowing his coat to one side.

"What is he waiting for like that?" whispers Pablo taking another sip of his drink.

"You'll see," John tells him.

Salvador's chin is tucked close to his chest as he finally crosses the street and arrives in front of the neighbour's house. He leans his forehead against the yellow door.

"What's he doing to the door?" Pablo demands.

"The woman who lives there is his lover, I think," whispers John. "The single mother with the child I was talking about earlier, remember?"

"Was I too harsh with him at the café?" Pablo takes his last sip of cognac and goes towards the kitchen for a refill.

"Of course," responds John. "You sounded like a preacher. What got into you, beating a man who's already down, like that?"

"I'm such an arse!" Pablo takes a noisy gulp.

"We know that. By the way, I think I have nuts in that cupboard over there. Eat some or you'll get drunk." He waves carelessly towards the kitchen as he glances across the street.

"That man's dying of grief . . . Look at the way he's leaning on that door."

Salvador straightens his back and stuffs his hands in his pockets, having rung the doorbell.

"Turn off all the lights, will you?" John motions to Pablo. "I don't want them to see us."

"That's the one I saw at the café with him!" Pablo whispers to John as the yellow door opens.

"Why are you whispering?"

Across the street, the woman is at the door, which she keeps ajar, not inviting Salvador in. She keeps looking behind her, towards the apartment, as if expecting to be caught any minute. Salvador reaches over to caress her hair, starting from the top of her head, following the roundness of it down to her cheek. The woman reaches for his chest and they remain there in quiet embrace. John moves away from the window, urging Pablo to do the same. They sit down on the old couch, still mesmerized by the tender sadness of the lovers in the dark doorway. Pablo is holding a jar of peanuts from which he is absentmindedly taking fistfuls and stuffing his mouth.

"What do you think he's going to do?" he asks.

John has no answer. Then, "I don't feel like going out." he says. "You want to make that spaghetti here?"

Pablo nods, looks at the jar in his hands. "I think I've eaten more than half the jar . . . You know, this whole thing has given me an idea for my next *Cosmo* article. Infidelity is a hot subject."

"Yeah, put some statistics showing men are immature jerks; add some expert quotes highlighting the role of testosterone, in their defence. I think I've already seen something like that in one of those magazines . . . "

"No, no. My article will be about women who go for married men. Is there a profile? Who are these women?"

"Good luck. So what do you need for the sauce?" John asks and opens the fridge. "Do you want to use this old smelly broccoli in it?"

Pablo goes closer to the fridge and sniffs. "Caramba! That's absolutely vile! When was the last time you cleaned this fridge?"

John has no answer.

"You slob! That broccoli should have hit the garbage bin two weeks ago. Guys like you give men a bad name!"

"Go ahead, blame my dirty fridge for not getting laid in the last decade!"

"I get laid plenty!" Pablo straightens, holding an empty pot in his hands.

"Uh-uh . . . And that's how you get time to iron your underwear."

"Shut up or I'll stuff that broccoli . . . "

"You know, Pablo; I've seen you in that café for so many years; corduroy pants, shiny shoes, endless political debates and all that. Suddenly, we're friends. You're criticizing my fridge, the broccoli etcetera . . . I'm really touched by all this. Seriously. Do you want more cognac?"

℮

Across the street unbeknownst to the two men cooking spaghetti in cognac-induced euphoria, Salvador is once again standing facing a closed door. He puts his hands in his pockets and walks down the street with his back hunched to counter the cold wind blowing in his face. He turns a corner and disappears.

℮

Later in the night, after Pablo's departure, John is walking around the apartment tidying up before going to bed when he notices something shiny on the couch. It's a keychain consisting of a small metal coil, with two keys attached to it, and it's lying on the side of the sofa where Salvador had momentarily sat. He picks it up and places it on his desk, near the picture of Jeannette Daoust, wondering if Salvador would return for them soon. He goes to bed, his mind floating this way and that incoherently, like a piece of cork in the open sea. The fisherman returns and once again John sees the baked shoulders and taut back as he pulls his oars, rowing away from the shore. John wants to wave for help but cannot move his arms. He is helplessly bobbing over the waves, his head dipping in and out of the water. The fisherman observes him from the side of his boat as it slides past. John feels hopeful that he will be rescued. But the fisherman looks up and away at the horizon. John glances down at his own body, revolted by the fisherman's snub, to find nothing but a piece of driftwood. He is horrified by this transformation as he floats farther and farther away from the shore, his extraordinary efforts to be recognized having miserably failed. He wants to howl his revolt, rage against his fate, as he continues to helplessly ride the crests; a piece of grey driftwood lost in an infinite mass of blue.

Of Salvador, there is no news for a while. He does not return for his keys and is a no-show at the café the next afternoon where John sips his café au lait, sitting with Pablo who complains of a hangover to the saxophone player, Ali, who in turn complains of meagre earnings playing at the Sherbrooke metro station. John goes back to work later in the evening as usual, and returns home in the morning on Bus 144, sitting right behind the Asian woman with her dragon purse. There is something comforting about such oddity, he reflects, as he descends from the almost empty bus and looks up to see her gazing at him from the window. He makes a mental note to pay attention to the days when she gets off before him and the days she remains on the bus after he gets off, to find a pattern.

When he arrives home, he once again stands by the window to see the woman and her boy leave her house. Instead, a swarthy, muscular man comes into view right outside his window. Next to him is a thinner, blond one who promptly rings his doorbell. They are both wearing navy blue parkas which make them look like they forgot to wear the rest of their uniforms. He opens the door. The thin man confirms John's identity and shows his police badge.

"We need to ask you a few questions, sir."

"What about?" asks John, keeping the door half closed.

"We're investigating a case," the dark one replies. "Do you mind if we come in for a moment?"

John retreats from the doorway to let them in. He invites them to sit down at the table.

"A woman has been found dead in an apartment in Notre-Dame-de-Grace. Her husband told us he was with you the night of the incident. His name is Salvador Rodriguez. Do you know this man?"

The blond officer has a note pad ready. He starts to write as John opens his mouth to speak.

"Sort of . . . "

"Were you with him the evening of March 27?"

"Yes."

"Can you tell us what happened?"

"I met him and Pablo, a friend of mine, in a café on St-Denis. We had coffee together. Then we decided to go have dinner at Pablo's. I needed to get my gloves so we came here, and then decided to stay here instead."

"Do you know him well?"

"No, I had seen him once before, but got acquainted that day."

The dark officer, named Constable Ayotte, asks him about his job, background, and life. Then he returns to Salvador. "Can you tell us the circumstances of your acquaintance with this man?"

"I went for a coffee. Pablo, who is a regular there, called me to his table, where he was sitting with Salvador. I joined them and Salvador started telling us about his dilemma. He was married unhappily it seems; he told us he loved another woman who wouldn't have him because he was married. I gathered his wife had a drinking problem. He seemed quite downcast."

"What time did you leave the café?"

"I don't know for sure. It was already dark outside. Perhaps six PM?"

"Tell us what happened then."

"We came here, directly, had a drink or two. Decided to stay at my place and prepare supper. He left about one hour or so later saying he had something to do. He crossed the street, to the apartment with the yellow door over there. She is his lover, I think. We saw them talk at the doorway and then we stopped looking. I don't know what happened after that . . . Later that night I found these keys on my sofa. I figured they must have fallen out of his pocket." He removes the keys from his pocket and shows them to the cops before placing them on the table. "Is he a suspect?"

The blond man stops writing, "We're interviewing everyone at this stage. There are no suspects. Can you tell us how we can contact this Pablo who was with you?"

"Pablo Mendes. He's usually at the Café Martine in the afternoons. Works as a free-lance writer."

After a few minutes the officers leave John's apartment and cross the street towards the yellow door. John sees the woman come out and talk to the officers; she is dressed for work in her coat and gloves, her arm around her son's shoulders. He sees her nodding, listening, squinting as they speak to her. He closes his blind and moves away from the window.

After a few hours of lying in bed with eyes open, he gets up and sits at his desk, looking at the picture of Jeannette Daoust next to Salvador's keys which he placed there after the police officers' departure. He opens his green notebook to the last page of Romeo Fournier's story, turns a blank page and presses it down with his left hand as he looks at the two objects sitting side by side on his desk.

He hesitates, pen in hand, before bending his head down to write a name, "Claire." He continues, "Her name was Claire," and although he wants to write about the neighbour across the street, he realizes Claire is the name of Salvador's wife. This is it, he thinks, every time I write something down, I end up writing something I never meant to. "So why is this about Salvador's wife, when I actually want it to be about the woman across the street?" He mumbles to himself as he gets up from the chair and lies down again in his bed, watching the ceiling until his eyes feel heavy with sleep. His mind drifts, his stomach growls and he wonders about cooks, last meals, and finally about a cook named Derek who prepares the last meals of those on death row somewhere in Arkansas. He forgets about Claire. How do you knowingly prepare the last meal for someone who is about to die? What if they want truffles and wild boar? Would they stay the execution until the truffles are found and sent? Would Derek pray before cooking? Would he weep over the truffles? A cold sweat gathers on John's forehead as he delves deeper into the story of Derek who literally holds in his hands the last pleasurable moment in the life of an unfortunate man. He sees this prison cook, a dark, paunchy man in his mid thirties, wake up at five AM in his small bungalow. He steps over children's toys in the dark to get to the kitchen as his family continues to sleep. He works for the state prison, like everyone else in that neighbourhood. The fence is somewhat discoloured, he notes, sipping his coffee at the window while the sun rises meekly in the horizon, colouring the dusty landscape with its bluish light. Something to do on the weekend. He quickly bites into an old soggy cinnamon bun and leaves the house, bun in hand, towards his old pickup truck. He drives to the prison listening to whatever's on the radio, some country music, perhaps something about the Lord. He parks his truck in the empty lot behind the immense concrete structure of the prison. Alone in the vast metallic kitchen, he goes down the list. Breakfast, lunch, and dinner menus for a few thousand inmates, plus the last meal of Jeffrey Banting, serial killer with an IQ of a six-year-old. Request: strawberry pancakes with lots of syrup and chocolate milk at 7:45 AM. Execution time: 10:30 AM.

John's eyes are wide open now, terrified as he is by his own imaginings. He knows somewhere someone is having this life, this death. He can almost hear the hollow breath of the sweaty, shivering man eating his last pancake soaked in syrup before breaking down into sobs, "Please dear God, please don't let them kill me. You know I didn't do it. I promise I'll be good . . . I don't want to die!" Jeffrey Banting, whoever he may be, whose simple-minded howling prayer now, as in the past, will rise unheeded.

~

He looks at his radio clock. It is 10:30 AM. He runs to the bathroom to wash his clammy face, wanting to retch. The telephone rings.

"Were you sleeping?"

"Who is this?"

There is silence on the other end. John wipes the water off his face with a towel.

"Who is this?" he repeats, trying to place the man's voice.

"Salvador . . . "

"Ah! Salvador, I heard this morning . . . My condolences. I'm so sorry . . . "

"They came to question you too?"

"They did . . . I think you dropped your keys here. I have them if you need them."

"My place is cordoned off. Can't go there until they finish investigating or whatever it is they do. Thanks, anyway. They didn't want to take them?"

"They should have, shouldn't they? Maybe they'll come back for them . . . Do you have a place to stay in the meantime?"

"Not really. I think jail, perhaps."

"Why jail? Did you do it?"

"I think they suspect me."

"But you left your keys here. How would you get into your house?"

Salvador sighs deeply. "They probably think she was alive when I got home, that she opened the door for me."

"Was she?"

"I think she . . . " he begins, " . . . anyway, what does it matter!"

"There is a Bed and Breakfast not far from here, on St-Denis. Maybe you can stay there for a few days?"

"Can I come over to see you?"

"Salvador, I . . . you know I work nights. I really must try to sleep before my shift. I can see you at the café around four . . . "

"Oh . . . Right . . . Sorry I awoke you . . . Bye."

"Salvador?"

"Yes?"

"What are you going to do now?"

"I'll figure something out . . . "

"No, listen. I don't think I can sleep much anyway. Come over, man. It's okay."

"You sure?"

"Yeah, just get here fast; I don't want to fall asleep in the meantime. It'll be worse if you wake me later. Tell you what, you come, and as long as I sleep three hours before work, I'll manage."

"I'll be there in a couple of minutes."

"Where are you?"

"Around the corner from your place."

Salvador enters the house with an entirely different countenance than that of the lithe, handsome man John had seen in the café. His blood-shot eyes are half closed, his clothes crumpled, the shadow of a dark stubble on his face gives it an ominous, fearsome look. *Raskolnikov,* thinks John. He looks like a murderer gone mad.

"You look awful," he says, unable to hide his shock.

"I wandered around all night. Walked all over the city for the last two days . . . Streets I'd never seen before. Can't seem to stop." He closes his hands together to stop them from shaking.

"Her eyes were open . . . " Dry sobs shake his shoulders.

John waits a moment for the sobbing to stop.

"Look, we'll talk about all this after you get some sleep. Looks like you need it more than I do. Do you want to shower? Shave?"

"Maybe . . . that would be good."

He hands Salvador a towel, pyjamas, an extra toothbrush from his closet. When he hears the water in the bathroom, he quickly places some sheets on the couch, prepares a glass of water with a sleeping pill next to it.

After the shower and shave, Salvador returns to the living room, takes the pill at John's urging and lies down on the couch in John's pyjamas.

"You're a kind man," he says before drifting off.

∾

76

John goes to bed in his room, a few feet away from the couch where Salvador sleeps. His door is open wide, so that he has a full view of the sleeping man from where he lies. He tries to keep his eyes open as long as possible, uncomfortable about having this man, a stranger until a couple of days ago, possibly suspected for murder, sleeping on his couch. He will call Pablo in a couple of hours to tell him about it, so that he won't be the only one taking care of Salvador. He finally drifts into sleep and awakens to a clanging sound. When he jumps out of bed and arrives in the living room, Salvador is no longer on the couch but in the kitchen, trying to make coffee.

"I hope you don't mind," he says apologetically, "I didn't want to wake you up. Thought I'd look for everything myself."

John nods, relieved. "Make some for me too, will you?" he says and goes to open the small window in front. He then picks up the phone on his desk and calls Pablo and tells him to come over.

"You got me a babysitter?" Salvador says and pours the coffee, trying to keep his hands steady. "Sorry I've imposed on you. Tomorrow I'll go find a room."

"Don't worry. I just thought you might want company for a while . . . Besides, Pablo would have spent half his day at the café trying to pick up women. He'll be more useful here."

"Do you think I killed my wife?" asks Salvador looking straight into John's eyes.

"I have no idea what you did. Do you want to tell me?"

"After I left your place, I crossed the street and went to knock on the yellow door over there. I didn't tell you that day, but I was quite disturbed to find that she lived across from you. I had to go see her. I couldn't bear it. She didn't let me in on account of her son being there. He doesn't know me and she's protective, naturally. We talked for a little while, then I got into my car and drove up to the mountain, and all round . . . Basically not wanting to go home . . . My days, you see, are full of elaborate schemes to avoid going home. So everyday after work—I'm an engineer by the way, I don't think I ever told you—I get into my car and drive around, visit cafés, restaurants, bookshops . . . that is, unless I can see September, your neighbour, which lately I haven't been able to do, as you know. Driving is good. I can just sit there and be in my own world as the landscape changes all around and there are no demands, no dilemmas, just music, turn right, turn left . . . "

He walks to the window with his cup of coffee. "Do you ever see her from here?"

John pretends disinterest. "Sometimes in the mornings when I come home, she's leaving for work. In the evenings too sometimes, when I go to work. Not often," he lies. "How did you meet her?" he asks, the name September now on his mind.

"She is my dentist's assistant. I needed fillings. If I didn't, I'd invent them, just to see her. She has a degree in anthropology. I've never understood that . . . Do you?"

"Yeah, sure I do," says John, "there are PhDs out there driving taxis. It's a Montreal thing."

"You're right," Salvador agrees. "I've had a few of those."

"So, what happened after you left us here and drove up and around the mountain?"

"I finally went home. It must have been close to eleven PM I don't know. It's a blur . . . I walked up the stairs to our apartment. I looked for my keys. That's when I realized I must have dropped them somewhere. But the door wasn't locked . . . Her arms were flaccid, hanging cold . . . dead, on the couch . . . "

"You called the police and they came."

Salvador nods and sits down.

"I'm sorry I brought it up; let's not talk about this any more. I mean unless you wish to . . . ," John says, as he waits for the bread slices to pop out of the toaster.

"No. I don't! It's a nightmare and there's no waking. No deliverance. It keeps getting worse."

"What are you going to do?"

"I'll have to wait till this gets sorted out; if it ever does. And then . . .

I have no idea."

John places toast, jam, and butter on the table in quick fluid gestures.

"Here's breakfast in the afternoon. You must be hungry in any case. Start eating. I'll take a quick shower and join you soon."

Standing under the hot water jet he wonders what the cause of death was, and whether her name was Claire. He cannot ask those questions and hopes Salvador will eventually volunteer this information. He steps out of the shower to shave quickly, cuts himself from all the hurrying and finally gets out of the bathroom fully dressed. Salvador is sitting sideways at the table staring at the crumbs in his plate.

"Her name is . . . was Claire. My wife. I always thought it suited her perfectly. Blond hair, French kind of beauty; there was always a scarf, something, elegant shoes, the very straight narrow nose and small ankles. She was lovely . . . I regret having said I didn't love her any more. I mean, she was my wife of sixteen years, you don't just stop loving . . . I simply grew tired . . . not knowing what to do, hoping she would do something to change. I worried constantly about accidents, public embarrassment, private misery. There was plenty of all that, all the time. This finally comes as no surprise . . . It's almost as if all these years she had been committing this long, slow act of suicide; you know? I kept blaming myself, thinking she drank because I didn't know how to make her happy, that I failed her somehow. She was in and out of rehab a few times. During one of those periods, she told me what she had never told anyone. Her secret. The damage. I understood. I stopped blaming myself for her drinking, but then you blame yourself for not helping more. You end up living this guilt-ridden life without ever knowing why you feel guilty."

Salvador, still deep in thought, sweeps the crumbs off the table with his knife and continues, "I hardly know you, John, yet here we are. You welcome me to your home, and I spill my guts out to you . . . "

The doorbell rings and Pablo walks in, bringing in a whiff of fresh, cold air, some moisture, and a duffle bag. "Salvador!" he whines and walks over with big thudding steps to hug the seated man. "I'm so sorry to hear of all this." He continues in Spanish, leaving John out of the conversation. John busies himself cleaning the dishes and putting them away, leaving the two men to their exchange. They do not notice him go to retrieve his navy blue packsack, lifting their heads only when he clears his throat to bid them goodbye for the rest of the night. Before opening his door to leave, he remembers to give a set of keys to Pablo and last-minute instructions. Then he is gone.

e

For Salvador to feel like a suspect, her death must have been suspicious, John thinks to himself as he advances towards the bus stop. Was there a firearm, signs of struggle? Perhaps, he thinks, my guest will tell Pablo. He goes over the entire scenario from earlier in the day, including his first impression upon seeing Salvador—that of a dishevelled murderer. There is a sort of excitement within, despite the grave circumstances, about being part of a dark mystery, something life-altering for people he hardly knew a few days ago. The lovely single mother across the street, her tenebrous Spanish lover in the café who inspired intense jealousy, pompous Pablo who brought them together, and now, an unlikely friend-ship emerging from the death of a woman named Claire.

A shudder goes through him as he boards his bus. The last time he shuddered, in precisely the same way, at the same spot, was the day he found out Romeo Fournier had expired. He quickly takes out his note-book from his packsack. *The River Oblivion,* he scrawls as his head bounces lightly on the bus window, *pulls away the dead from our world of memories towards unknown shores. Who remembers you now, Romeo? Where has your suffering gone, the thrills of your soul? Where do the sounds from your throat echo now? Who hears them? Are they taken by the same wind that caresses the river?* He stops, trying to suppress his tears. He shuts his notebook quickly, but when morning comes, it brings its own torrent of remembrance, and this he cannot stop. He wipes his wet face with his coat sleeve, watching the afternoon sunlight retreat from the bustling street like the hem of a long skirt behind a closing door.

Every life distils into something. Something tangible that will not be carried away by the currents of oblivion, but will remain there, a stubborn reminder of all things ethereal. Like human life. Like the soul and its movements. John feels he is reaching a profound conclusion, as his mind focuses deeper into this thought. Darkness has descended blankly upon the streets, pulling his gaze towards the traffic lights, the moving automobiles, the stiff mannequins in store windows. The bus keeps moving, taking the daydreaming John beyond the hospital, where the road is now flanked by dark silhouettes of trees. When he realizes he has missed his stop, he pulls the chord vigorously as if to alert the driver to something more urgent than a planned stop. The bus slows down and stops at the cemetery. John gets off, annoyed by his distraction, and prepares to cross the street to take a bus back towards the hospital. Waiting for the light to change, he turns towards the quiet graveyard and on a sudden whim, starts walking there. The wrought iron gate has been left ajar, dark fir trees stand noiselessly among multitudes of white marble headstones. Thawing mounds of snow make the occasional muted thud, shifting their masses. Thousands of headstones, rows of glinting grey in the moonlight . . . a city of the dead, where the paths are for the living. He walks upon the wet frozen dirt, gazing at the tombstones, each with an inscription, a name, a lifespan. Here the journey to oblivion begins.

"Once your words filled the air. You visited this cemetery aimlessly, like me, not considering you'd come to stay. Now your stones have wilted flowers for company and you are no longer present."

He speaks out loud, urged by a desire to hear his own voice in this strange solitude.

"You, Sylvain Bonenfant, and you, Gertrude Beauchamp, are neighbours now, and you don't even know it. Even your children are dead . . . The city is down there, unconscious; the houses where you were born, the streets where you played. I hope you weren't stingy, Sylvain. I hope you gave generously, because from the look of your grave you could have afforded it. Did you have a large nose, ingrown toenails? Sylvain, you old fool . . . Here you are now, visited by someone from across the ocean, unknown to your grandchildren, if you have any . . . "

As he continues to palaver freely, he hears a rustle from behind one of the tombstones.

"What are you, a prophet?" A man's voice crackles from behind a tomb. "Or a lunatic?"

The voice breaks into a deep phlegm-ripping cough.

John freezes in his spot, sweat gathering on his brow.

"Who is there?" He inquires meekly.

The cough subsides and the voice answers gravely, "I'm a voice from the past. I've been sent by Sylvain to prove you wrong."

John shakes his head in fearful disbelief as he slowly advances towards the tombstone that speaks.

He reaches over to see behind it, trying to keep his teeth from chattering.

A young man, not older than nineteen, is sitting on his coat, which is spread out like a blanket on the frozen, muddy ground. His left sleeve has been rolled up, revealing a pale forearm squeezed by a rubber band above the elbow. A bloodied syringe lies beside him on the coat. His greasy blond hair is parted in the middle, falling on his shoulders like wilted lettuce. The large red flashlight on the ground illuminates sunken cheeks on an angelic face.

"Dear God!" exclaims John in disbelief.

"For a moment, I thought you were an atheist there, listening to your speech about the dead," the young man smiles, his eyes unfocused. "Funny how we tend to call for God when we least expect it . . . " His eyes roll up behind his lids, leaving the whites of them glaring at John for a moment.

"You need medical attention. Let me take you to the hospital."

John kneels next to the boy, removing the rubber band and pulling the eyelids back, holding the flashlight in his face.

"Hey, you don't need to save me, Nurse Ratchett. I'm fine here."

"Nurse who? Come on, get up, lean on me."

He tries to pull up the young man, who lets his body weight pull John down. They struggle, John watching the bloody needle from the corner of his eye, trying to steer away from it as he lifts the boy up. He carefully wraps the needle in the boy's coat while leaning him against a tombstone and stuffs it in a plastic bag which he removes from his packsack.

"The nurse from that movie . . . aaah . . . with Jack . . . aaah . . . what was his name . . . can't remember. The American actor . . . Fuck . . . Jack, Jack . . . "

"Nicholson?"

"Yes . . . That's it. So in this movie, they put him in a loony bin, and there's this nurse, right? Nurse Ratchett . . . Yeah . . . They lobotomize him in the end . . . "

"I see," John says as he pulls the teenager along towards the gate.

"Why are we talking about that anyway?"

"No idea . . . "

The boy suddenly remembers.

"I'm not going anywhere." He stops and turns around to go back.

"Let's get out of this place; I'll buy you a coffee. We'll wait until you feel better and talk. If I leave you here you'll freeze to death."

"So what? Florence . . . Florence . . . Fuck, I can't remember any of the names . . . "

"Nightingale."

"Yeah, that's it. You're a pretty smart guy. Where are you from?"

"Down the street. And you?"

The boy stops in his tracks and begins to laugh.

"Oh, you're funny!"

"I can't say you are."

"Hmm . . . " He continues walking next to John, leaning on him slightly.

"Was that heroin?"

The young man does not answer.

"Do you usually come here to do this?" John asks again.

"Yeah . . . " .

"Odd choice," mumbles John as they walk through the gate.

"They don't object. And they don't try to help." He waves his hand towards the graves behind them.

"Where do you live?"

"Somewhere down the crazy river . . . ," the boy sings.

"Do you have a home?"

"I preferred it when we talked about movies. You sound like the police . . . " He stops, trying to steady himself, face up to the sky, eyes closed.

"Are you feeling faint?"

"No. I'm feeling high."

"Do you have family here?"

"Family is fucked up, man."

"Is that right?"

"Yeah."

"Why?"

The boy stumbles as they cross the street, then steadies himself in the middle of the road and stands there trying to think. John pulls him along to the other side with great effort, feeling the sweat gather around his collar, under the wool scarf.

"What was the question again?" asks the young man, letting himself be pulled along.

"What's your name?"

"What's yours?"

"John."

"You can call me Ben."

"Ben like Benjamin?"

"Ben like Benoit."

"Now, we'll take the bus. How much of that stuff did you inject?"

"Who knows?" Ben shrugs, giving a blank smile.

"How long have you been doing this?"

Ben shrugs again.

"Where the hell do you find the money for this stuff?" John mutters as he leans the boy against a street light to remove his scarf.

"I live in a big house," Ben says unexpectedly.

The bus arrives and John pushes Ben onto it, grasping his jacket from the back. He puts in two tickets and leads the boy to a seat. The boy holds his head back, his eyes closed, looking ghostly. John keeps talking to him.

"Do you have a cell phone on you?"

The boy indicates his pocket.

John stretches over and takes the phone out. "May I?" As he dials, he keeps his eyes on the unresponsive youth, his fingers expertly looking for a pulse on his wrist.

"Anne? Yes, I know I'm late. Got a boy here, high as a kite, I'm bringing him in. Can you go down to triage and meet me there? We'll be there in five . . . Never mind, I'll tell you later. Bye."

❧

When they arrive at the emergency room, Anne is there, waiting. She takes the boy's vitals. John removes the plastic bag from the coat and carefully discards the contaminated needle.

"Where did you find him?"

"I missed my stop, ended up in the cemetery, where he was shooting himself up."

The pale boy opens his eyes. "You forgot to tell her . . . you were speaking to tombstones . . . "

Anne looks at John and gives a smile. He quickly reacts: "Just look at him, he's almost in a coma and still talking nonsense!"

❧

Anne pricks Ben's inner arm for a vein, to start an IV, as John takes down his incoherent history punctuated with bursts of coughing. Benoit, it turns out, comes from Outremont, where wealthy French Canadians with old money live in large stone houses with manicured lawns. His father is a lawyer and the boy indicates he has no fixed address, having left home a while back. Doesn't remember how long ago. He started experimenting with drugs and alcohol at the age of twelve. He refuses to give the name of his father or next of kin. Finally, after some prodding, he provides a woman's name, an aunt from Lachine, Gisèle Boivin. He signs a few forms and an authorization, with a shaky, childish signature. John asks if he can call her and the boy nods, before his eyes roll up, leaving the whites to stare at John as before. The specialist arrives, John hands him the chart and leaves the room.

Gisèle Boivin's raspy voice comes to John's ear in the form of a recording. From her voice, intonation, and type of accent he imagines her look. Very skinny, hair frozen into a bowl with a spray. Pants ironed with sharp creases. Smokes Du Maurier regulars. A pack or two per day. False teeth and a very bony, square jawline. Slightly bulging large blue eyes. Fifty-three years old.

He leaves a reluctant message in French to call the hospital regarding her nephew Benoit.

When he returns to Ben's bedside, the boy has an oxygen mask over part of his pale face and his eyes are closed. The nurse has taken blood for testing and is wheeling her trolley away. The heart monitor beeps at regular intervals. Looking at the immobile face, a picture darts through John's mind of Ben eating cereal from a bowl as a small child. A tiny, serious face, hair the colour of sunshine, alone in a quiet kitchen, teeth crunching on the cereal carefully gathered from a milky bowl with a large spoon, while thick flakes of snow descend on the window sill outside. The image vanishes, leaving John to wonder how he got from that cereal bowl to this hospital bed. There is always a story, and this one, he suspects, may never be told.

e⁓

He sits at the bedside, gazing blankly at the heart monitor. Why this job? Why this life? He looks once again at the boy's face, thinking he would tell Ben his own story if he opened his eyes and looked at him. He waits for a while, in suspense. Ben's eyelids remain shut. John's desire to tell his story recoils. Careful not to make a sound, he rises and leaves the neon-flooded room.

e~

When he boards the bus in the morning, exhausted from the events of the night, he goes over them in his mind once more. Ben's aunt, who arrived at the hospital at eleven PM with her husband, looked nothing like his imaginary picture of her. She was a portly brunette with pudgy hands and her husband looked like a Gaul, with tufts of white mustache hanging down like brooms from both sides of his mouth. "Mon pauv' 'tit Benoit!" she had exclaimed, running to his bedside. As he lay unconscious she was told he had AIDS, acute pneumonia, and heroin addiction. It was as if she had been punched in the face. The woman stood there shaking her large head and repeating to John that there must have been a mistake, her nephew Benoit could not have gotten those things.

John awakens from his reverie when the old Asian woman with the faded dragon on her bag pulls the cable to signal her stop and descends at the corner of St Lawrence holding a couple of plastic bags. After the bus has moved on, John notices the embroidered cloth bag sitting shapelessly in her seat. He wants to tell the driver to stop so he can run after her, but the woman is no longer visible. John gets up and takes the bag in his hand, hesitating between giving it to the driver and keeping it in his packsack until the next day. He finally takes it with him as he gets off, squinting at the early morning light shining into his eyes.

His apartment is empty when he arrives, Pablo and Salvador having left for the day to let him sleep. He enters and walks to the window, out of habit, realizing he no longer expects to see September. He wonders how that story will end, whether Salvador will be cleared of the suspicion over his wife's death, whether he will start a new life with September and her small boy, creating the family he seemed to have yearned for most of his adult life. As he tumbles into bed, he thinks that would be the first happy conclusion to have crossed his path in a long time. He closes his eyes, patiently waiting for the fisherman in his creaking boat to make his appearance once more. Instead, he finds darkness. The simple and absolute darkness of his eyelids telling him to shut down and let go.

He stops hearing the street noises, the water drops hitting the kitchen sink at monotonous intervals, and the seagulls announcing the arrival of spring in their shrill, querulous squawks. He drifts off peacefully in the comfort of his bed, feeling the melancholy oppression of the world slowly lift from his chest.

ℯ

Across the Atlantic, in a small Swedish town, Arvid Lundsgard has finished eating his afternoon snack of butter and jam toast and is quickly licking his fingers on the sly in lieu of washing hands, while his mother is walking to and fro with busy determination. It is raining outside and they are making ready to leave the house for the airport, where Fru Selma, the owner of the swing and the farmhouse, is about to get off her plane. Fru Selma, a tall lady with sad eyebrows and freckled cheeks, always brings him the same chocolates from the airport; the kind he does not like, with raisins and nuts stuck inside like rabbit poop.

His mother has repeatedly warned him to take the present and thank her and be quiet. Arvid suspects Fru Selma herself is fond of these odd-looking chocolate bars embedded with raisins. Why else would she give him such unattractive candy? He muses that adults complicate chocolate the way they complicate life with their rules. From this thought he concludes that while his mother keeps reminding him that she too was once a child, it is not at all evident from the things she does and therefore this is merely a parental tactic meant to fool him into acquiescence. A lot of his mental energy is spent thus figuring out how to unravel adult deceptions surrounding his childish universe.

The exciting thing about this morning, however, is putting on the shiny raincoat and boots, with the prospect of watching airplanes land and take off, and later the swing in the fragrant garden of Fru Selma's farmhouse.

He stands patiently as his mother zips up his coat and helps him into his boots before ushering him into the pouring rain. Rain batters the windshield as mother and son drive to the airport to the familiar tunes of Vivaldi once more. Arvid wishes his mother would listen to something else on rainy days, as his eyelids get heavy, lulled by the moving car, the rhythmic swishing of the wipers, and the strains of soft classical music. He has barely enough time to revisit his two major grievances before drifting into profound, mouth-hanging sleep: raisins in chocolate and hypnotic violins.

Fru Selma arrives at the busy airport filled with strangers and echoes of repetitive, unintelligible instructions blaring out of hidden speakers. Arvid sees her before his mother does, gaily sauntering towards them, holding a large cloth handbag and a colourful plastic airport bag which he hopes contains pure milk chocolate for him.

Her orange hair is loose and bouncy around her freckled face. He sees slivers of gold shining through her blue eyes for the first time as she bends to pick him up and give him a peck on the cheek. She smiles and reaches into her plastic bag with that conspiratorial wink adults like to give children. He sees the lilac wrapping of his favourite milk chocolate and gleefully exclaims, "Mama, look! No raisin-poops!"

The two women smile at his childish outburst as they begin to walk towards the exit, pushing the cart laden with the lady's luggage. Arvid tries to stuff his present in the pocket of his raincoat when a curved, cardboardish piece of paper brushes his fingers. He takes John's forgotten photograph out of his pocket and hands it to Fru Selma before placing the lilac package back into his pocket. Fru Selma stops in her tracks.

"What is it?" asks Inga.

Selma shows her the picture.

"Where did you find this, Arvid?" Selma asks.

"In my pocket."

"No, before you put it there . . . "

"I don't know. Can I have a square of chocolate now?"

"Thank you, Arvid," says Selma, having recovered from her surprise. She turns to Inga, "This was the picture I was looking for when I called you."

"I have no idea how it got into his pocket. Perhaps he found it on the floor the day we came to look for your things. So, what are you going to do now, Selma?"

"We'll go to my house and have coffee, first. Then I'll think about it. The kids will come in a few months when their school closes. Maybe I'll paint the house . . . I'll grow a few things. Buy a horse?"

"You seem well," Inga observes.

"I'm mostly relieved. My marriage . . . It was over long before this. I mourned its passing for many years, while we were still together. Now I'm done. I feel sad for him, though. He hasn't accepted it, even though . . . " She sighs, before continuing, "the women, the constant travelling . . . Anyway, I'm here and it's over." She nods with a sad smile, casts a sidelong glance at Inga at the wheel, and then at Arvid listening to their conversation with wide open eyes.

"So, Arvid, tell me, is the swing still in good condition at the farmhouse?"

Arvid nods.

"You will come often to swing in it, I hope. It's yours any time you want. Just tell your mom you want to come."

Arvid nods gravely, wondering what the two women were talking about. It sounded serious, like someone had died.

"Who is the man in the picture?" he asks now.

"An old friend, I guess," Selma's reply comes out, hesitant.

"What's his name?"

"John."

"Where does he live?"

"I don't know. Canada, maybe."

"Where is that?"

"On the other side of the Atlantic Ocean. I'll show you on a map when we get home."

"Why do you have his picture?"

"As a souvenir."

"What's a souvenir?"

"Something, an object, that you keep to remind you of a person, a place, something that happened long ago. It reminds you not to forget something important."

"What does this picture remind you of?"

"Arvid! Stop interrogating Fru Selma."

"It's okay, Inga. I really don't mind. It reminds me of a time when I was much younger. It reminds me of seagulls and the smell of a boat in the sea. A sunny day when I said goodbye to my friend and felt sad."

Arvid shakes his head.

Selma, who has been holding the photo on her lap lifts it up and looks at it once more.

"Is he dead?" Arvid continues asking.

"I don't know."

Inga presses the button to play her CD.

"Mamma! Not that song again," whines Arvid.

"I thought you liked it . . . "

"I hate it! It makes me sleep."

She lowers the volume a little and Vivaldi's music fills the moving car, effectively putting an end to Arvid's conversation with Selma. Arvid sulks, gazing at the passing scenery, telling himself that he will resist the urge to sleep this once.

Selma also gazes at the passing scenery, the pine forests interrupted by meadows and the steeple of a church rising in the distance, announcing a town, on the way to the farmhouse. The snow has thawed entirely, giving the earth a dark, muddy brown colour. The trees, still bare, stand in unison, awaiting the sudden explosion of leaves and colour within a couple of weeks. The car swerves onto a dirt road, and the old familiar thrill returns to Selma's heart, knowing she is approaching the farmhouse and her new life in the midst of fond childhood memories.

Later, alone in the house, she stands the curved photograph against a vase in the living room and proceeds to carry her suitcases up the stairs. The house is quiet except for the creaking of wooden floors under her feet. The great expanses of meadows and forests enters her vision through the surrounding windows. She knows it will not be easy to make a new life for herself here, the sadness of her failed marriage already permeating her view; her husband's loosened tie hanging sideways the night she announced to him her departure, the children's hurt eyes avoiding her gaze at the airport. *What have I done? What have I done?* Tears stream down her cheeks as she continues to climb the stairs, tightening her grasp on the suitcase handles.

In another time zone, on the island of Montreal, John feels a tightening in his chest before opening his eyes from his daytime sleep. He does not remember the dream that may have caused this sensation, but as he gets up slowly and walks away from his crumpled bed, Selma is on his mind. Not Selma in person, but his aching for her. The hollow space within, named after her, which has grown wider in time. At first, it had felt like a bridge that would enable them to find each other one day. Then the bridge became a burden, a link to places one never visited, something that stood in the way of moving elsewhere. Years later, when he observed the new landscape within, he found no remnants of the beloved bridge; only the gulf that had made its existence necessary. He took to living his days on the shores of her absence.

He rubs the sleep off his eyelids, begins to fill the kettle with water. Could one call this a life, this dedicating one's days and hours to the loss of hope? Days like the beads of an abacus, pushed to the other end, one by one, counting towards nothing. Like Romeo Fournier, the cobbler, who for decades had spent insipid holidays in various parts of the world dreaming of running into his lost beloved immortalized in a torn photograph, John aches for the woman who will never again materialize for him to behold. The night job is about wanting to sleep off his days, and the hospital gives his ache new faces, new reasons to remain anchored in his heart, perhaps. It is not often one perceives the inside of one's soul in such sharp outline. The thought is already fading in his mind as he sits down at the table waiting for the water to boil. The doorbell rings.

Pablo enters carrying grocery bags, followed by Salvador's shrunk silhouette.

Pablo has a magician's way about him, John muses, making pregnant silences disappear instantly from one's mind. He leaves no room at all for doubts or fantasy, occupying the air with garrulous prattle.

"Have you slept enough?" he asks now as he goes towards the kitchen with the bags. "You may have noticed that your fridge smells considerably better. Salvador and I cleaned it after you left yesterday. Have you opened it yet?"

John shakes his head. "I just got up. Was making tea . . . "

Pablo empties the bags in quick, efficient movements. "We shall eat coq au vin tonight. How does that sound?"

"Complicated," answers John.

"But pleasurable . . . " retorts Pablo as he pulls out a bottle of red wine. "You sit over there and let me handle this."

"Pablo," interjects John, "are there ever days when you do nothing at all, when you don't even shine your bloody shoes?"

"Let me tell you a story, my friend . . . Years ago when I got off the plane that brought me here from Buenos Aires, I left the tarmac on one of those funny little buses with chimneylike extensions thinking, 'Pablo Mendes, you foolish bastard, look around you! You are now at the Mirabel International Airport. The futuristic portal to your utopian city of Montreal.' I picked up my suitcases, got into a taxi. Passed through green flatlands that went on forever. In my head was an image of Montreal designed like this airport. It is funny, isn't it, the city you picture in your head versus the city you find? Well, anyway, after I got out of the taxi and into my hotel room at Queen Elizabeth, a kind of melancholy filled my mind. I stood somewhere on the fifth floor of the hotel, looking vaguely towards the McGill campus, at people walking to and fro, crossing streets. Everyone busy out there, pretty women in floral dresses, and Pablo Mendes alone in his air-conditioned room surrounded by generic hotel furniture, having floated away from any kind of meaning. 1979. I ran away from the junta into this moment of utter . . . alienation. That night, I walked along Ste-Catherine Street with its drab little shops overlooking sidewalks congested with people. Everyone was on this street, but it was impossible for me to figure out why. I got into a movie theatre. Seville. The floors creaked. I thought I saw a rat. They were playing *8 1/2* by Fellini . . . Anyway, that was the most important night of my life. I either had to find the new Pablo within or perish from the unbearable sadness of life in exile. So, here you have me, dear friends. I shine my shoes every morning in memory of my first night in Montreal."

He's smiling as he removes the raw chicken from a transparent plastic bag, placing it on a cutting board. He washes and dries his hands, uncorks the wine bottle, pours wine into three glasses. He walks over to Salvador and John who are sitting on the sofa farther away, silently considering his story, and hands them their glasses before lifting his. "To shiny shoes!"

The other two also lift their glasses, not entirely convinced. John proposes another toast. "Here's to Salvador. May you find peace."

Salvador offers a tired smile and takes a gulp. "Thank you both for not letting your suspicions get in the way of your enormous kindness. I will never forget this." He takes another gulp.

"I did not kill my wife. I say this to you in all honesty. There was trauma to her head, they say, but I have a feeling it happened from falling down and hitting it on the metal wine rack. They did determine she was so drunk she could have been comatose. I was able to get into the apartment because she had not locked the door; she never thought to. I was always the one who locked the door at night. Even if she got in at four o'clock in the morning, I would get up and go lock the door after her. I had the car that day, so she must have either gotten drunk at home, or elsewhere, and taken a taxi home. When I arrived, she was already dead and I was too shocked by the sight of her to go looking for clues. There was blood on the side of her head, it had run down her cheek, and there was a smear on her hand. I've been trying to recreate what happened in my mind since that moment. I'm unable to do anything else . . . I suspect she fell, hit her head and touched the bleeding spot. She managed to rise and went to the couch, where she expired, because that is where I found her. The blood was already dry, so I figure at least an hour or so must have passed between her accident and my finding her." He pauses, and takes another gulp of wine. "It's awful, but I had to tell you this. I need you to trust me. I already feel too much guilt about my marriage and what happened to it, to also feel the burden of your suspicions." He looks at Pablo. "You are lucky, Pablito, you shine your shoes everyday and it works for you. I don't know what will, for me."

Pablo lifts his eyebrows, remains quiet. The three men take sips of their wine in unison.

"I better start this coq au vin if we are to eat if before John leaves. Do you have any music around here? It would help me work."

John goes to his CD player, which has CDs stacked up all around it. He plays one.

"Ah, Piazolla!" exclaims Pablo. "Very thoughtful of you!"

Salvador goes to the window and stands gazing at the yellow door across the street.

"Shall we invite the neighbour and her kid over?" John offers.

Salvador is not sure.

"Why not?" interjects Pablo. "You're neighbours aren't you?"

"I don't think this is a good circumstance for introductions," replies Salvador. "Perhaps next time . . . "

"We don't need introductions. It's a neighbourly invitation. That's all. We certainly won't talk about the . . . or anything like that. Something light-hearted. Why not?" John insists. "Come, let's go knock on her door."

He opens the door, waits for Salvador to follow him. They cross the street. Salvador knocks on the yellow door. September appears, looking confused.

"I think you know my friend Salvador," begins John, "he is staying with me for a little while, and so is my friend Pablo, who is making us coq au vin. We thought you might want to join us for supper with your

95

son . . . Unless you've already had supper?"

September hesitates. The little boy has also come to the door. John introduces himself and his friend to the boy, who offers his hand politely for a shake.

"When should we come?"

"It is 4:30 now. How about at 5:30? I start my shift at 7:30, so it'll be an early supper if you don't mind."

"That's fine," she smiles. "We're used to eating early." She puts her hand on her son's head protectively and caresses it. "I'm September, by the way and this is Eric."

℮

Back in his apartment, John taps Salvador's back, feeling pleased with himself. He asks for Salvador's help to put some order in the apartment before the guests arrive.

"What do kids that age like to do?"

"I don't know, maybe play?"

"Yeah, well, I don't have any toys, as you can imagine."

"Maybe a movie?"

"How old is the kid?"

"I think he's five or so . . . He'll probably bring some toys of his own."

"Salvador, I hope things eventually work out for you two."

Salvador gives him a restrained, bitter smile. "Honestly, I don't think she wants to have anything to do with me any more. But thanks anyway."

Pablo has finished working in the kitchen by the time the doorbell rings, and mother and child enter with shy reserve. She hands John a bottle of wine in a crumpled paper bag and shakes his hand. Salvador walks over and gives her a peck on the cheek and shakes the boy's hand. Pablo in his exuberant style takes the woman by the arm, walks her to the kitchen, uncovers the pots while she nods, and explains the recipe with hand flourishes. Meanwhile John uncorks the wine and brings the glasses. Salvador is sitting on the couch a little farther away from the small boy, who has a plastic bag on his lap, his legs barely reaching the end of his seat. They both look awkward and silent until Salvador finally turns to the child and says, "Are there toys in your bag?"

The boy nods, taking a quick peek inside.

"Do you want to show me?"

He nods again and opens the bag, reaching over to Salvador. Salvador takes a quick peek into the bag at the assortment of small toys, pencils, and books and asks the boy if he can look at the books. Eric obliges, handing them to Salvador, who starts flipping through the pages of a book of cross sections. He observes the cross section of a tank, with all its minute details and mechanisms, including its small metallic toilet bowl.

"How fascinating!" he exclaims. "I'm an engineer," he tells the boy. "I'm always curious about how things work and how they look inside. This is fabulous, to look inside a machine, a vehicle, or even a building this way, isn't it? I especially like the toilet bowl."

The boy smiles. "Look at this one, there's a castle and you can see the cesspool with a guy shovelling poop."

Salvador smiles back. "What a job! I bet if they'd asked him as a boy what he wanted to do when he grew up, he wouldn't have said 'I want to be the guy who shovels the cesspool.' "

"Maybe his father did too," says Eric.

"Hmm . . . So, Eric, what would you like to do when you grow up?"

"Shovel the cesspool."

Salvador's eyes open in surprise at first, then he gives a smile before his laughter echoes through the apartment, filling the empty corners and bouncing off the furniture. It comes out in waves from his throat, arresting everyone there in mid action.

"I didn't think he knew how to laugh," says Pablo to September.

"That was a joke!" Salvador continues to chuckle, stroking the boy's hair.

John eyes September observing Salvador with her son. She looks pained, he thinks. She has written him off, yet sees how good it can be to have this man in her son's life. A family. She pines for a family. When she turns her head, she finds John gazing at her and looks down, blushing.

e⁓

When they sit down to eat, with Pablo serving the plates artfully and filling up wine glasses, the ambience in John's apartment is entirely different from the one he's been familiar with. This is not the place where water drips monotonously from the rusty faucet, where silence is interrupted only by the irritating noises of inanimate objects forced to work. She pines for family, I pine for this. For an end to self-imposed exile from day life. He lifts his glass.

"To the cook, for a wonderful meal, to you all for bringing life and comfort around this table."

They all lift glasses and clink them. Eric, with his orange juice and small hands follows suit, sitting next to Salvador, his chosen adult for the evening. September is sitting next to Pablo, who keeps her occupied in conversation on the other side of John, who listens quietly to all the voices around the table. He catches occasional glances travelling across the table between Salvador and September. John's heart sinks, there may be less hope now than there ever was when Salvador's wife was alive. Claire's death, the absolute silence of her story, appears to have become an insurmountable obstacle between them. Salvador has not been accused of anything, and therefore has not been exonerated of anything. He can tell his version over and over; in the absence of Claire, there will always be a lingering doubt in September's mind. *What if he killed her to be with me? What if? What if?* Then, of course, is *his* guilt, having wanted to get himself out of his marriage and not knowing how, and finally, his wish coming true in the strangest of circumstances. September, perhaps wanting the wife dead in the obscure, unspoken corners of her heart. Sometimes you get what you wish for, thinks John, and you wish you hadn't.

Unexpectedly, Salvador clears his throat and announces in his steady, melancholy tone, "Friends, I have thought a lot about my life in the last few days . . . After my wife's funeral and the formalities regarding her passing away are dealt with, I will move to Halifax. There is much that I love in this city, close friends like you that I shall miss. But this chapter is done for me and I want to start anew, elsewhere. I hope you will come and visit me there." He raises his glass and takes a sip, all the while looking into September's eyes. "I hope you will," he repeats softly, and looks down at his plate.

September's shoulders shrink a little as she puts her glass down and in turn gazes at her plate after glancing at Eric quickly. Eric, oblivious to the scene, is eyeing his plate as well, for something attractive he can start chewing. The chicken with its muddy wine sauce is not very appealing to his eyes, so he gingerly fills a spoon with white rice, which seems safe to eat.

"What's in Halifax?" asks Pablo, taken aback.

Salvador smiles sheepishly. "I have no idea. It's far enough . . . "

"Don't you think you need to know something about a place before moving there?"

"Pablito, you knew nothing about Montreal when you came here. Did your ignorance stop you?"

"Fine," says Pablo and nods, attending to his plate.

e⌐

Later, when September and her son have left and John has dashed off to work, Pablo stops washing the dishes and bursts out, "What was that nonsense about Halifax, hombre? The woman is here, what will you do over there? You just about ruined my chicken!"

Salvador shakes his head. "It's not so simple. She will always have doubts about me. This is done, do you understand? Finished."

"Have you spoken with her about this?"

"Don't you see the way she looks at me?"

"Looks can always change. What you need is time, not huge distances. This woman has a kid, responsibilities . . . If she wants you, do you expect her to pick up and go across the country like this? What are you, stupid? She probably can't even afford the bloody ticket to go visit!"

"If she does do it, then we will both know she's gotten over all this and has overcome her doubts."

"This is getting worse . . . So, this is some sort of test? For her?"

"No, chico! Why are you being obtuse? As long as I'm here, she won't get over this thing. If I leave, it'll give her time to reflect. Plus, my leaving helps exonerate me a little in her eyes, don't you think? If I . . . killed my wife just to be with her, moving to Halifax is the last thing I would do, right? I'd rush and marry her and be done with everything. Whereas I am moving away . . . Trust me, this is the only solution left to save this thing. Besides, I cannot live here any more. I have too many memories of this place that I would rather forget, can't you see?"

Salvador's pressed speech comes to an abrupt stop and he starts to ponder quietly.

"Salvador," says Pablo slowly, "if you didn't do it, then you shouldn't worry about her thinking you did it. If you didn't do it, and you know it, she will know this too."

"Pablo, you're a good man, but you know nothing about these complications."

"All I know, Salvador, is that by trying so hard not to look guilty, you will end up looking it."

"Look, she broke up with me before my wife died. Even if she wanted to, she will never allow herself to be with me now . . . because of guilt."

Pablo is unconvinced. "This woman just wants to be happy, I think. Life hasn't been so kind to her so far, right? It is very unfortunate about your wife, but given time . . . "

"I don't think we can pretend away what happened."

Pablo shakes his head, thinking all this to be rather senseless in his view, and tells Salvador he's going out for a bit of fresh air.

℮

While Salvador sits pondering his options alone in the apartment, across the street, at the far end of the corridor behind the closed yellow door,

September sits at her desk in her bedroom, gazing at the backyard from her window. The old wooden terrace has softened with rot all around; broken, sunken pieces of it giving way to bright green weeds and thorns bursting into life from their winter stupor. Through the glass of the closed window her reflection comes back to her, somewhat distorted and faded over the wild greenery and dark brown wood barely visible at this hour. *I, my ghost, and a small dark jungle filled with centipedes who find their way into my bathtub, grasping onto the discoloured enamel with all their legs, waiting there until a frightened scream moves the air around them, once again setting their multiple thin limbs in motion. The faucet is turned on with groping fingers, quickly, quickly! The child is still screaming. A plastic bowl is filled with water and the shiny brownish centipede is washed away, gurgling its way into the hole, down the pipe, threadlike legs curled and shivering in agonizing confusion. More water. Hot water. Lots of it. Drown it. Away with the insolent crawler who's crept in from the wild. Look, it's gone. Don't worry. It won't bite. Just looks ugly, that's all. Why so ugly, why?*

℮

A shiver goes up her spine and shakes her shoulders. Some things cannot be answered. What is there to say about ugliness for which there is no cure? *It isn't ugly, actually. It just looks so different from us that we find it repulsive.* You live with them long enough, you stop screaming or shivering at the sight. You still drown them, to be sure. Not the Dalai Lama. What does he do, the Dalai Lama? Make a grimace and try to put the thing into the plastic bucket to go and shake it off into its habitat, unharmed? Would he make a grimace, or not? That is the question. Does the Dalai Lama suppress his repulsion in order to do the humane thing, or does he actually feel no repulsion, only all-encompassing love for a fellow creature reincarnated as something that lives in rot and creeps into empty bathtubs with its many threadlike legs and long antennae which move this way and that, chilling our warm-blooded spines into convulsion. A centipede that has lost its way, entering white, slippery enemy territory, where insect legend tells of the gurgling rush of scalding water, or the sudden flattening of limbs under a giant object. The place of no return. There is no cure for ugliness.

⁓

September rises from her desk, walks towards the bathroom to brush her teeth. She turns on the light and inspects the bathtub first. Spring is the season of such mishaps. She wishes for higher wisdom whenever she runs into centipedes, and apologizes for flushing them down the toilet. Reincarnation is not a plausible conjecture. Regardless, the desire not to harm something living is within her, she thinks as she brushes her teeth, except for germs and bacteria. The Dalai Lama once again visits her idle reflections. What is his take on germs, bacteria, and such? Does he refuse antibiotics from fear of interfering with their right to live? This whole thing is way too complicated, she concludes, as she reaches her upper molars awkwardly with her brush and then spits white foam down into the sink, rinsing and gurgling before turning the light off. Not before a second inspection. Then she walks to her son's room, turns the light on quickly, checks the walls and ceiling for possible enemy incursions, and turns off the switch as soon as he starts moving in his sleep. She goes back to her room after checking the lock on the street door and prepares her clothes for the next day—an ironed white uniform which she folds carefully and places into a plastic bag. She would not wear this thing in public, even if it means wiggling in and out of her clothes in the small washroom where her boss, the dentist, has just done his Number Two. Quite vile that stench, and no fan to take it away. She sighs, feeling humiliated, and takes her clothes off. When she finally lies in bed thinking of Salvador, she is surprised he took so long to enter her mind. She lingers on the pleasurable Salvador moments in her life, knowing he will soon leave. She wants to postpone this thought, lest it cause more heartache. Still, she reflects, there's already much of it. She did not doubt his innocence when the police came to interrogate her. She does not believe him capable of murdering his wife. He is not a man to grasp a blunt object and hit his wife on the head. Salvador is not like that. His eyes penetrate through her defences, eyeballs, teeth, skin, blood, and organs, and touch her where she is most vulnerable and true. The places where she is like no other, where she stands alone in her raw nakedness. This is how she could not resist Salvador. This is how it entirely broke her inside to turn him away. There will never be another like him. She knows this. But one does not live life in raw nakedness, and she does not even know whether she can ever inhabit the other realm of daily tedium with him.

"Mommy, I had a nightmare!" whimpers Eric at her doorway.

September lifts her cover and he rushes into her bed in practised movements, rolling into it like a ball.

"It's okay," she whispers and kisses the back of his head, before falling asleep. What moves in her chest to come out as a sigh is a strand of melancholia, a soft thing ripped from its roots, floating up into the waves aimlessly, never to be owned again.

℮↷

The phone rings around three in the morning. She lifts up the receiver, coming out of sleep, and does not make a sound. At the other end is Salvador, whispering.

"I'll be at your door in a minute," he says and hangs up. She gets out of bed, taking care not to move her son, to find Salvador waiting at her doorstep.

"What?" she whispers.

Tree branches, still naked, sway noiselessly outside. There is a rolling can somewhere, the distant meowing of a cat, traffic on St-Denis, an ambulance, the lingering smell of garbage and urine. He pulls her outside by her arm and holds her against the wall. She pulls him in, and closes the door so that they remain in the hallway between two doors, their hands moving urgently, fumbling with fabric, as they continue kissing until he lifts her up around the waist. They sway and turn in their awkward waltz until he breaks into sobs, frozen in this embrace, his chest pulsing into hers.

e~

A few kilometres away, on the fourth floor of the west wing, John walks into a patient's room as an airplane crosses the sky over the city. From the airplane window, passengers arriving in Montreal observe the large castle glimmering in the midst of a dark forest on the hill, among all the tall boxy skyscrapers filled with electric light.

e~

Inside the plane is a businessman in his early fifties who has loosened his tie, letting it dangle sideways. He sits inclined, one leg thrown over the other uncomfortably, and winces as the plane accelerates its descent. City lights appear as the plane swoops lower to reveal speeding cars on serpentine highways. The view from a plane rarely reveals human life; it merely alludes to it. The businessman straightens himself in the seat and fixes his tie, knowing that soon he will walk out, briefcase in hand, towards passport control, then out to the cold air in search of a taxi. He has taken the long trip from Greece, having put his two teenagers on a plane to Sweden to visit their mother. One more business trip. He anticipates handshakes in uninspiring square buildings surrounded by geometric lawns and clipped shrubs, expensive lunches and drinks where only the most insipid details of life will be exchanged amidst forced laughter, and solitary nights watching TV, all the while knowing there is no home back home. Montreal could be Athens for all he cares, and his own bedroom means no more to him than the one he is about to enter swiping his plastic card. He throws back the cover and lies down in his suit, having left his briefcase right beside the bathroom door.

e~

He is still unable to grasp how his life crumbled overnight. His married life, his family, the home they called their own, the unit that once was. It wasn't the best, it was not even adequate probably, but it was. And now it all seems like an illusion, something he invented to torment himself in foreign cities. How easy it has been for Selma to disengage herself from it all and leave him to carry the weight of defeat. She was prepared, as one who suffers a muted and lengthy withdrawal from love. She had been wounded by marriage, he intuits now, whereas he had callously ignored the deeper layers of it where her happiness bled away. He reconsiders callousness for a moment, not finding its use kind to his person. Many times he observed this incongruence between them. Her thoughts consisted of unexpected thrusts which he did not care to fathom; she sought harmony where he only found gears, she told him once. The affairs, he realizes momentarily, were perhaps his way of finding equilibrium. Under control, was the word. Her fluttering mind he could not order, but her space, he could, in a way. And did. It kept flying—her mind did—into invisible barriers until it could no more. He was enamoured with her enthusiasm, and spent their marriage extinguishing it because it would not do, because he could not handle the chaos of her spontaneity.

*

Thomas sighs, exhausted by the long trip and his unusually harsh introspection. His wrist watch beeps, reminding him of his reason for being here. He rises to open his laptop, starts looking at emails, charts, and various figures. Soon it is all gone, the soul-searching; and order reigns once more in his universe of gears.

*

John, a few blocks away, has opened his green notebook while munching on his square mortadella sandwich. The juice box, apple, and yogurt are lined up in front of him. Anne passes by, staring at the careful arrangement of food on the desk.

"You line up your food like a kid at lunch break," she smiles. "This is cute, Johnny!"

John's face colours as he looks up at her. "Habit," he mumbles, looking down.

"My brother used to do the exact same thing, when we were small. He ordered them on his desk from least favourite to favourite.

Sometimes we played naval battles and such, with lunch food. It would have never occurred to me. I just looked forward to eating." She giggles.

John points his finger, "Yogurt is favourite, juice not." He smiles. "You called me Johnny."

"Did it bother you?"

"No . . . I hadn't heard that in a very long time, that's all . . . "

"The green book is out. Thought you'd lost it."

"No time. Things just kept happening. Ben?"

"Checked out. He was in no shape, but he wanted to leave." She hurries away in her white running shoes. Her uniform is pink today. John focuses on the blank page. Nothing happens for a while. The page is unyielding. He keeps chewing at his bread, flipping the pages back and forth, hoping the movement itself will bring the thought back. There was one, before Anne's interruption. He can no longer trace it. He closes the cover and opens the packsack to put the book inside. He tries to stuff it in, but it doesn't fit. He opens the sack wider. The red dragon bag lies shapelessly at the bottom of it. The corners are worn, the fabric has thinned into shreds. Unable to resist his curiosity he opens the bag. There are a few small, stained white cards with Chinese characters on them. He picks one up and flips it over. MY NAME IS LIU. He picks up another one and looks at the back. HOW MUCH? Another card appears to have her address, somewhere on Clark Street in Chinatown. There is also a smaller purse of black cloth inside. He undoes the metal clasp to find a five-dollar bill folded a few times and some change. There's an embroidered handkerchief at the bottom of the bag, unused. There are a couple of black hairpins, crumpled cash receipts, two small metallic balls supposed to help with arthritis. A small plastic photo album with transparent sleeves. Seven pictures. In one, the old lady is standing beside a stylized stone lion at the entrance of a hotel or restaurant, with a four- or five-year-old boy whose straight ink-black hair is cut to perfection all around his head, looking like a down-turned bowl. The old woman is somewhat younger in the picture, perhaps five years, holding the same red bag. It looks like they are about to enter a restaurant for dim sum. They are smiling, squinting in the sunlight. Another photo is a black-and-white touched-up portrait of a woman, from the fifties, possibly. The back is stained with age. The third is an old faded colour photo of a diminutive young woman in a red silk outfit, her face powdered and ghostly, her red lipstick painted in the form of a cherry. He figures the picture is probably from the sixties. He closes the picture book and carefully places it in the bag.

My name is Liu. How much?

He wonders how long she's lived in the ever shrinking Chinatown. When he arrived in Montreal years ago, it seemed to him like Chinatown was a decrepit part of town, with old men and toothless women shuffling on the sidewalks in padded jackets, holding small bags. Ming, a Chinese friend, had explained to him that the wide avenue next to it was there to prevent the encroachment of things Chinese into the downtown Montreal core. Over the years, the few blocks that remained of Chinatown got refurbished, an attractive oriental gate was built at the edge of it, inviting the Quebecois bureaucrats working in the unsightly grey and brown towers to have authentic Asian cuisine in quaint Chinatown. Ming explained that there were two menus in Chinese restaurants, one for white ghosts who didn't know how to eat, and another for the Chinese, who could order on a small piece of paper in Chinese characters.

MY NAME IS LIU.

HOW MUCH?

He stares at the cards absentmindedly. *The details of a stranger's life have a way of bringing back one's own.*

"Why are you nodding?"

Anne has curled her brown hair, he notices. It looks fluffy, bobbing every time she moves.

"What happened to your hair?"

"Curlers." She puts on her glasses, having sat down.

"A date?"

"Not really."

"And so?"

"A girl can't change her hair? Do I need your permission now?"

"Knock it off. It's nice, I meant. You should do it more often."

"Liar, you just think it's weird."

"A Mohawk cut . . . I'd think it weird. This is, what's the word . . . feminine. Oh look, you've painted your nails pink, too! Something's up, Anne! This, I've never seen before."

"A couple of old friends are coming to visit from PEI. Haven't seen them in a lot of years."

"An old flame among them?"

She blushes instantly. "Mind your own beeswax!"

She rearranges her glasses and picks up a pen.

"Fine," John, says, feigning nonchalance.

"He's coming with his wife and daughter."

He sits up.

"It's been a lot of years. We were practically kids, when . . . I bet he doesn't remember anything."

"Why are they coming?"

"They've never been here. They'll go to Ottawa, Quebec City. Just visiting . . . You know."

"Know his wife?"

"Know of her. Not personally. It's been something like fifteen years, John. A lot of water under the bridge . . . "

"Hmm." He's not convinced. He puts the rest of his supper back in his packsack and gets up to do his rounds.

"What is your life like, John?" Anne hesitates, before continuing, "I mean, when you're not working . . . You don't have family here, I figure. So for instance when it's a holiday and you don't come to work, what do you do?" She stops, looks away. "I don't mean to be nosy or anything . . . "

e๛

John sits down again. "I have friends I go see, I have coffee here and there, wander around, sit in bookstores, write in my notebook."

"Don't you get lonely?"

"Sometimes. Don't you?"

"Sure. Often, actually. I sometimes think I should go back home. But when I think harder, I give up. After so many years, all my friends have gotten on with their lives, you know, kids, husbands, whatever. You?"

"What?"

"Do you ever think of going back?"

"No." He gets up. "Time for my rounds," he announces and goes to get his trolley. "Remember the old man who didn't know where his wife was? He died a while back. Romeo Fournier . . . "

"Yeah, what about him?"

"Who's in that room now?"

"Not sure. Wait a minute . . . " She looks through the charts. "An elderly lady. Very small frame. Asian, I think. Doesn't speak much English."

"Since when?"

"Since yesterday. Picked up by ambulance after a 911 call, shortly after 8:30 AM. In Chinatown. Motor Vehicle Accident . . . multiple fractures, soft tissue injuries. What else? She had no ID on her, it seems. We have no name, no age. Was taken to St-Luc Hospital but they sent the ambulance this way. Overcrowded. So far, no one's been to see her. Why did you ask?"

"Don't know . . . I still think about the old guy, sometimes . . . Room 417?"

Anne peeks at the chart. "That's right."

John rolls his trolley down the hall and stops in front of 417. The door is open. The patient's curtain is pulled back, so that in the dim light he can see the small child size frame lying on the bed. Strands of her long grey hair fall upon the pillow. One of her legs is in a cast and hanging from a chain. He walks in to take a closer look. Her eyes are closed.

"My God! It's her . . . ," he whispers, recognizing her. The bed loses its sharp edges and begins to float. He leans on the night table to steady himself. Her heart monitor keeps beeping steadily. *"My name is Liu. How much?"* he whispers. She opens her eyes momentarily and moves her lips silently.

"Pardon?" he asks.

But she's closed her eyes again, is motionless.

Behind her lids it seems to her that there is a light behind a red curtain. She remembers her fingers around a lit lantern; the transparent redness of them. She would like to open her eyes but can't, the lids are heavy and won't move. She knows the pale face with the black hair. She knows it well. From where? Her mind tries to grapple with the question. The moment passes, and the face fades away.

"Aaaoooh . . . "

This is all John hears, a soft moan.

"Mrs Liu?"

Mrs Liu does not hear him.

She is somewhere familiar, a place with mountains with sharp contours and greenery that falls off the edges abundantly. She knows this place too, but it will not name itself to her. She is in a realm of intimate mysteries where she recognizes the things she cannot remember. Her nostrils are wet from the mist in the valley. There is a lake upon which an old wooden raft advances, the oar making a splash that echoes around the mountains. The water is stretched flat like a glass pane until the oar dips into it, disturbing its surface. How fortunate to have returned to this place, she marvels, and I never thought I would see it again. Am I in heaven? The jingles of a multitude of tiny bells approach from somewhere behind her. The sound echoes around the hills before coming to her ears amplified. She knows if she turns around she will see goats, white goats herded towards her by Xiao. She does not want to turn around yet. Xiao, she remembers. Apple-faced Xiao.

"Liu!" he calls her, and the mountains echo her name. The raft is halfway across the lake now.

"Liu . . . Liu . . . Liu!" Her heart swells thinking of Xiao behind her, surrounded by his white-bearded herd; she knows she will soon see his ruddy cheeks, the chapped lips that glisten in the morning light, the plump hand on the walking stick, smelling of goats. She does not turn around. She wants to hear her name again, and feel the touch of his hand on her shoulders, nudging her lightly before she turns around to face him. "Xiao, Xiao . . . " she repeats in her mind, anticipating the sound of his name on her lips. It will reverberate in her mouth, this wondrous name, seep into the light, into the misty forests around the lake. The mountains will echo it. She tilts her head sideways coyly, and turns to face him, light shining in her eyes. He will know how much I love him when I straighten my neck to look at him. He will know from my voice repeating his name that he is all there is to love.

⟨∾⟩

She looks up. There is a greyish haze, a man's bony white face with crow black hair flopping to the side.

"Go away! Ugly!" she exclaims. "Ugly!"

She closes her eyes again, emitting a faint whimper.

John moves away from her bed, wondering whether the adjective was meant for him or someone in her dream.

⟨∾⟩

She wants to return to the lake where Xiao awaits. All she sees are the insides of her red eyelids, the ruby curtain lit by a lantern. I'm an old woman, she remembers. Xiao is dead. They married me to Merchant Wu when I was sixteen and he was fifty-eight. I was his second wife. He forced himself upon me night after night. I knew nothing of all that. Ugly. Merchant Wu was revolting. I thought of Xiao when Merchant Wu was done with me and I wept. I had three children with ugly Wu and wept. He died of a heart attack in a brothel at the age of sixty-eight. I was so happy, I wept. Never saw Xiao again. Never saw the face that gave me joy. Xiao is dead. I'm waiting to die here, among white ghosts. My grandchild, Xiao. I want to see my grandson. I have wept all my life. Maybe I am dead. I hope I am in heaven. Who is that white ghost with black hair? I know him. I know him . . .

John notices the fluttering eyelids. He approaches the bed once more.

"Mrs Liu?"

She opens her eyes wide and says something he doesn't understand.

"Do you speak English, Mrs Liu?"

"Who . . . you?" she frowns.

"I'm the man on the bus. Man on bus. I found dragon bag. I am man on bus." He gesticulates.

"You speak English bad," she nods. "Who . . . you?"

"I, John," he points at himself with both hands. He corrects his speech quickly, "I am John. I work here at the hospital. You had an accident."

"Accident?" she asks, her eyes widening. "You . . . kill me?'

"No! No . . . you hit by car. Me, work at hospital. Me, work here." He points at himself and at the floor. "Me take Pine Avenue bus with you."

"Me take bus, now?" she looks at her hanging leg in disbelief. "Me stay here. You take bus!"

The stupid man is the white ghost from the bus. I remember him now. What does he want from me? I don't speak English, but I think he can't either. He wants me to take the bus?

"No, no," tries John again, frustrated. "You had an accident. A car hit you on the street and you were brought here by ambulance. Remember? I work here. You understand?

"Every morning I take the bus and you're on it. Right? It's a coincidence. You left your bag on the bus a few days ago. The dragon bag. I have it. I'll bring it to you shortly. Okay?"

He looks at her, awaiting her response.

"Many English . . . " She stops, her face morose.

"Accident. Boom. You, here. Me, here for work. I take care of you now. Right? I know you from Bus 144, Pine Avenue. Every morning. You there, me here. You with dragon bag. Me with packsack. I have dragon bag, you forgot it on the bus. I'll bring it to you now." He stops miming, feeling tired.

"Where . . . my daughtah?"

"I don't know. You want to use the phone?"

"No numbah. Numbah at home."

"Daughter in Montreal?"

"No."

"Great!" He leaves the room, muttering.

"Daughtah in Vancouvah!"

So, he stole my bag, she thinks. Now he pretends he found it on the bus. I knew he was up to no good sitting behind me on the bus, staring at me, every morning. I'll check my bag when he brings it. Maybe he thinks I'm senile. He probably took my money.

℮

John walks up to Anne, asks her to find a translator. "Mandarin, Cantonese, probably. At least it would be a start. I was jumping up and down like a monkey in there. Don't know how much she understood. She said she has a daughter in Vancouver. Doesn't know her number. We'll have to get exact names and everything. Can you look into it?"

He bends down, rumages inside his packsack, and retrieves the discoloured red dragon bag.

"What's that?" Anne asks.

"You won't believe this story . . . This old lady is on Bus 144 every morning when I go back home. She forgot her bag when she got off last. I picked it up thinking I would see her on the bus again, to give it back to her the next day. Instead, I found her here. And now I'll give her the bag."

"That's odd."

"Hmm. Poor lady, though. Hell of a way to get your bag back!"

"Odd things always happen to you. Don't you find it really weird? I mean, you see her on the bus everyday, she loses her bag, you find it, she ends up in this hospital on this floor . . . Or, like that kid in the cemetery. Such things never happen to me . . . "

"You don't take the bus," he says. "You drive a car, alone, across the bridge and park it underground. Then you drive back home, alone, across the bridge and park it underground. The only thing that could happen to you is a traffic jam."

"I can't take buses any more. Takes forever."

He starts back for room 417.

"You make it sound like I lead such a boring life because of my car," Anne says.

"No. *You* do. Besides, there's nothing weird about what happened to me. It's another kind of routine. That's all. I don't get stuck in traffic jams. The smell inside a car makes me nauseous, so there . . . You know the fish market on Pine? When people get on the bus there, it smells fishy all over. I hold my breath or get off. I'm lucky, I live close to work."

"I think there's a nurse in the maternity ward that speaks Cantonese. Let me go ask." Her large brown curls bob around her shoulders as she walks towards the elevator.

ℯ

Mrs Liu has fallen asleep again. John leaves the dragon bag on her night table and tiptoes out. She moves her head away with a moan. She is with Merchant Wu again, not having succeeded in going back to the lake with Xiao. It is dark in her dream, the atmosphere grey and pale in the moonlight. Merchant Wu lies sleeping, his fat belly rising and falling as he snores. She has three girls. Only girls. He accuses her daily of wanting to ruin him by having girls. The two older ones are sleeping in the other room, together. The last one is two years old, in a small cot next to her bed. She does not like her children. They remind her of Wu. They even look like him. At twenty-five, she is already the mother of three. Almost four, and the last one might have been a boy, but she got rid of it. Wu never found out. She wants to get rid of that pouch inside her body into which Wu leaves his sticky wet seeds that grow into children who look like him. She gets out of bed, wrapping a shawl around her shoulders, and tiptoes out of the room, down the hall and into the fresh night air. She walks up the hill surrounded by dark mute houses and towering trees that bend and swish in the wind. She hopes to catch her death in the cold night air, for this torture to end. She rushes down to Xiao's lake and sits by the rocky shore, gazing at the large white globe hanging in the night sky, shivering. "Liu . . . Liu . . . Liu." Xiao's whisper comes to her, spreading into her bloodstream, prickling her skin like a thousand needles. The wind blows a goat-smell to her nostrils. "Xiao," she whispers back, the sound of his name spoken in her voice quickening her pulse, tugging at her womb. "Xiao . . . " She turns around and opens her arms to the goatherd. He sits next to her, apple-faced Xiao. Ten years have passed and he is no longer apple-faced; but her love sees only the sixteen-year-old boy when she touches the smooth golden skin of his muscular arms. She wants him in all the places soiled by Merchant Wu, on all the small bruised pieces of her skin. Xiao knows this. He knows he cannot make her happy as he kisses her nipples and softened belly in the gentle moonlight. Whenever they make love silently by the lake, she sobs, sadness rolling out of her lungs and into his chest in waves, only to be muffled by his embrace. This is all he can do for her. Bring out her tears and appease her pain. She will not run away with him. Liu lingers in his naked embrace, not wanting the dream to take her forward where Xiao must die. She feels the weight of his chest pressing down on her breasts, his gaze locked into her eyes as he caresses her hair. The blades of grass beneath her hips flatten tenderly, the willow tree above sways this way and that, lowering its branches to conceal their limbs. Liu feels loved by Xiao's lake and its whispering reeds. She knows it is time for Xiao to die now, as his lips seek hers. They kiss, and his back arches bringing a groan out of his chest. Blood drips onto her face out of his parted lips. He places his head into the hollow of her neck gently, whispers her name, "Liu . . . ", and is gone. Liu knows she is screaming but fails to hear her own voice as a hand pulls Xiao's head by the hair and removes his limp corpse off her naked body, throwing it aside in a heap. She sees the knife sticking out of his back; then, Merchant Wu's large crazed eyeballs crisscrossed with veins. Wu pulls her up to her feet by the hair and drags her home, naked, to the dark and grey bedroom where he lay snoring not long before.

⁃

Mrs Liu opens her eyes once more. She is in the same hospital room. Her heart is racing, and she is breathless. Merchant Wu never went to jail. He knew everyone that needed knowing. They said Xiao had been killed in the night during a drunken fight. No one questioned the knife in his back, his naked body. Wu beat her daily, threw her across the room like a sack, called her names, as the girls cowered behind the doors terrified. When she saw her frail children, eyes wide open in terror, looking at her bruised and swollen face, her affection for them awakened. They were from her womb, she reasoned. They were hers, more than his. In her womb grew Xiao's child. Another girl. The one who gave her the apple-faced grandson, Xiao. This fourth girl Wu never saw, having died in the arms of a whore. The day he died, Liu wore her red wedding dress and painted her mouth like a cherry. She went to a photographer to have her portrait taken. She left Wu's girls with her sister and took a boat to Canada with Xiao's baby in her arms and Merchant Wu's small fortune hanging in a pouch around her neck.

She never wants to remember these things, but they keep coming back. She wants to remember her daughter's phone number in Vancouver, to tell her to come and take her. She has few years left to live, and she wants to be close to her love child, Jiang, and Xiao. Jiang does not know she is not the daughter of Wu. Nobody knows this. What Jiang knows is that her father Wu died before she was born. Her mother had to leave her three sisters in China and come here, to Canada, to make money and send it home. She could not leave the baby back there, so she took her along. Jiang was told that her father Wu was kind, and he herded goats. She knew that Liu was so heartbroken when he died that she did not eat or sleep for weeks. The only thing Jiang found curious was her mother's insistence that she call her son Xiao. Liu begged her daughter to give him this name and would never say why.

Her foot hanging from the chain is itchy and far from her hands. She wonders how long they will keep her in this contraption. She turns her head to the side and finds her shapeless dragon bag. Reaching over with difficulty, she picks it up and brings it to her side on the bed. She takes out the small black purse within, where she keeps her money. It still has the change and the carefully folded five-dollar bill. She finds the small picture album and takes out the picture of herself with little Xiao taken a few years ago, the morning they had dim sum. At the back is the address in Vancouver and the telephone number. She presses the emergency bell beside her bed. Anne comes in shortly.

"Black hair man, please," Mrs Liu says.

"Are you okay?" Anne is annoyed about the bell.

"I got Vancouvah numbah," the woman smiles, "black hair man, please."

As Anne turns to leave, Mrs Liu has another request, "Foot itchy inside, need scratch!"

"Well, it'll stay itchy for a while, and you can't scratch. Please don't use the emergency buzzer again, unless you have an emergency."

"This, emergency!"

"Medical emergencies only. Like if something hurts, or you can't breathe. Okay?"

"Okay. Send black hair man now?"

Anne nods, and goes in search of John.

"The old lady found the Vancouver telephone number in her bag. She asked for you. With the emergency buzzer, no less!" She emphasizes the last sentence to show her displeasure. "She thinks it's room service."

John smiles to appease her and heads towards Room 417.

*

"Here, numbah! Call."

Mrs Liu shows him the back of the photograph. John picks up the photograph and dials the number. An answering machine comes on with a man's voice. He hangs up.

"Do you want to leave a message? There's no one home . . . "

"Call."

He redials and passes the receiver to her. She waits for the beep and goes into a long explanation in Chinese. She hangs up, pleased.

"Why you sit behind me, on bus?"

"I don't know . . . Well, why not?"

"Big bus, empty. You sit behind me. All time."

"I didn't notice."

She says something in her language, nodding.

"Pardon?"

"You strange man . . . "

"Mrs Liu, you always frowned in the bus. Here you're in pain, but you smile once in a while."

"Huh?"

"Frowning on bus. You."

"You sad, white ghost. I scared . . . Show me how dial numbah, now."

He shows her how to use the bedside phone.

"Thank you," she says. "Goodbye." She waves, to make him leave. As he turns the corner to the hallway, he hears her dial once again.

℮

In the farmhouse near Stockholm, the telephone rings. The black apparatus is sitting on a small antique desk at the entrance of the living room where a fire is spreading its orange glow on the wooden furniture. A boy is lying on the couch, listening to music with his earphones. He is about fifteen. He does not seem to hear the phone. Selma runs down the stairs for it. When she picks up the receiver, she is out of breath.

"Hullo!"

"Selma . . . How are you?"

"Fine . . . Thomas. And you?"

"I'm in Montreal. I thought I'd call before going to lunch. Are the kids there?"

"Yes, of course. I'll find Margaret for you. Here's Robert."

She puts the receiver on her chest and calls Robert, who does not hear. She reaches over and waves at him until he finally sees her. He lifts one earphone slightly.

"Your father. Come speak to him."

He gets up from the sofa, removing his earphones.

"Faster. It's long distance. Hurry."

She is annoyed by his newly acquired nonchalance at everything he does. Margaret is outside on the swing. Selma pushes open the new sliding doors to the veranda.

"Aren't you a bit too big for it now? It's for Arvid's size, you know . . . "

"I'm still only a teenager, Ma!"

"And this is a pretty old tree. Maybe we should get one of those sofa swings, with springs and such. We can lie down and swing and read. Your father's on the phone."

Margaret gets up to go indoors, sulking.

Selma looks in from the window at the silhouettes of her two teenagers side by side, the boy taller than the girl by about ten centimetres. She wonders how they sound to their father when they speak. *Will they get used to this space here? Will resentment against this house in Sweden linger in them when they are older, when they have lives of their own?* She breathes out a sigh. Robert has yielded Margaret the receiver. He opens the sliding doors and comes towards his mother, his limbs moving awkwardly, as though they found the rest of the body lying in bed one morning and picked it up.

"So," she smiles and ruffles his hair. "How's Papa?"

He squirms. "Okay, I guess."

"What's he doing?"

"Business."

"Do you wish you had gone to Montreal with him?"

"Not really."

"Come for a walk with me; we'll hike in the woods. Shall we wait for Margaret?"

He nods, not entirely convincing.

They watch Margaret through the glass, as she nods and speaks on the phone.

"Do you hear the silence?" Selma asks the boy. "This is what I missed the most, being away from here. The pure sounds of things being themselves."

He stares at her.

"At first you're lonely, bored, you wonder what there is to do all day . . . You're restless. Your mind doesn't know where to go. Then, one morning you find yourself sitting on the swing, or the porch, and looking at blades of grass. At first you're looking there because your eyes followed an ant, some bug into the greenery. Then you lose the bug, but your eyes remain fixed and your mind begins to expand over this tiny blade of grass. You're not thinking of anything in particular. It's a very passive way of being, you know. It just comes over you, the contemplation of things being themselves. It happened to me every summer when I visited my grandmother. At first I talked nonstop, telling grandma everything that happened to me during the year. Then things slowed down, even my eyesight. I'd be able to observe sunlight, how it touched things and spun around them; where it shone, where it drowned. And the brook over there. Can you hear it?"

He shakes his head no.

"I can always hear it now. I never knew it even existed. One day I heard water roll over smooth stones in the distance. At first I thought it was my imagination. Then grandma showed it to me. That is where I want to take you."

Robert's face looks different when he listens. His chin gets pointy and his eyes turn languorous as if he's diverting all his energy to his ears.

"Are you feeling tired, Robby? Your eyes look tired."

"Just listening to you, mom. I like your stories . . . How come . . . "

He stops, his eyes look down.

"Go on," she urges.

"How come . . . you often tell stories about your grandmother and this house but you never tell us much about your parents, mom?"

"I don't?"

"No. I don't remember any stories of them. You don't have that many pictures either. I always imagined your grandma was your ma."

"Hmm . . . I adored my grandma, that is true. I loved my parents too, but differently I guess. Because they were my parents. I wish you had met them."

"How were they?"

"My father was very busy. Kind of like yours, travelling and working late. When he was home, he was mostly in his study, working. We moved a lot . . . My mother, she liked high society. She liked dinner parties, playing bridge with her friends, always going somewhere else where I wasn't allowed to go. What I remember most vividly about her is watching her sitting at her dresser, in the evenings, putting her makeup on, choosing her dainty satin purses to match her outfit, her shiny earrings. She was beautiful. I used to watch her and think she was not made of flesh but something perfect. I always figured someone like that could not get sick or die. You'd think it would reassure me. But it didn't; I worried that she was illusory, that she would vanish."

Margaret is standing behind them, having finished her conversation with her father.

"What are you talking about?"

As she turns around to face her daughter, Selma anticipates the face she will see. The slightly raised eyebrows, the two pimples between them that she awkwardly tries to conceal with teenage makeup, the upturned smile of her soft plump lips, the look of shyness in her eyes belied by her set mouth. *My little Margaret.*

"About my parents. Robby thinks I don't talk about them enough. Let's take that walk now, we were waiting for you."

"Is it far?" Margaret asks.

"It's a good walk, I guess. Why?"

"Aren't you afraid it might get dark in the woods, and what if we get lost?"

"We won't. Stay if you prefer."

Margaret would rather stay, but will never fall behind if her brother can do it. She thinks of her brother enjoying his walk alone with mom, looking mature. It will not do.

She starts walking ahead of them.

"This way," calls her mother. As she turns around to follow them, Margaret has a slightly sheepish look in her eyes. She now walks behind the two.

"So, mom," she says now. "How did they die, our grandparents?"

"They were on a trip to Germany. They had an accident on their way back home."

"Where are they buried then?"

"Nowhere . . . " Selma shudders imperceptibly.

"Why?"

"It was a plane crash."

"Sorry mom."

Selma nods.

"Where were you?"

"Back home, it was the end of summer. I had just said goodbye to my boyfriend. He was going to Canada for good. He left and a few days later they died . . . Anyway, how about we go up here?"

She points towards a dirt road, which crosses a meadow before disappearing into the thick shady woods.

"How did you meet my dad?"

"I sort of knew him all along. He was a business associate of my dad's. He helped me a lot through those times. I was suddenly alone in the world, except for my grandma, who was out here and could not help me."

"Mom?" Robby asks in his uneven voice.

"What?"

"Why did you never tell us about this before?"

"How could I tell small children about a plane crash, losing my parents? It would have been scary. Besides, I suppose I wanted to get away from it myself."

They are walking along the dirt path in the woods blanketed with fragrant pine needles. Selma stops, taking a deep breath, and says, "The air is making me feel lightheaded. It's funny to think you can feel faint from too much oxygen."

"What happened to your boyfriend in Canada?" pursues Margaret.

"Who knows? He wrote me a couple of letters at first, and I never responded. The letters stopped and, well, who knows . . . "

"Did you love him?"

"I was young."

"But did you?"

"What a lot of questions you ask! I think it's not the clean air but your questions that are making me dizzy!"

"Mom?" Margaret does not let go.

"I did, I suppose. And now let's enjoy all this, shall we?"

"Mommy," persists Margaret, "didn't you want to go and join him in Canada, if you did? Love him, I mean."

"I met your father, he was there for me and I fell in love with him. That's it."

Above the tree tops, the sky is darker by a shade, turning purple.

"Looks like you didn't love him that much either," says Margaret, in a murmur.

Selma knows this sentence was waiting to come out all along. She can either pretend not to have heard, or respond. She tries to decide which as she takes one more step forward.

"That's not fair, Marg" Robby says in a low tone, having turned to face his sister. "Leave mom alone."

"I know you're both mad at me for changing your lives. But don't you think it's better for everyone this way?"

"I want one home. Not one in Sweden and another in Greece. Besides dad is not happy. Only you are."

"Look Marg," Selma takes on a more decisive tone, "you know us as parents, but we're also a couple and if that doesn't work we cannot be good to you either, because we become so preoccupied with our unhappiness, do you understand? We all have to learn to live with this new arrangement and find what's good in it."

"Whatever!" says Margaret now, sounding bored.

"What does 'whatever!' mean?"

Selma wishes her voice could have come out evenly, not edgy; it wants to scold.

"It means you'll say anything to make it right, so you won't apologize. I don't care!"

"Is this about an apology? I apologize then. I do!"

"No, Mom. It's about before the apology . . . It doesn't matter anyway, does it?"

"Of course it matters. You two matter to me more than anything. I would have stayed, if I thought it was better for you. But I felt our unhappiness was poisoning everyone's existence. You know, mom always looking dull, father always at work, and you thinking family is the place where everyone feels miserable. How can I expect you to find meaning in this world later if I sit and live meaninglessly myself? This is really hard for me, too. But it means something. It means I'm trying to find a way, I haven't given up. It means I have a heart and it actually beats into life rather than beside it. You know?"

"Why couldn't you find all this with him?"

"I don't know."

Selma feels the excitement that had just risen within her deflate.

"I just couldn't any more. I'm sorry."

The stream flowing over stones is clearly audible now, she can smell the water.

"It's over here."

She leads them through the foliage to a small stream running over a bed of rounded stones, occasionally eddying around larger rocks with a constant gurgling. Dark brown branches have fallen over it, gathering moss.

Selma sits down on a rock and quickly takes off her shoes and socks.

"Do it. Take 'em off."

She plants her feet into the cold water.

"Aaah!"

She sits back down on the rock, looking at her white feet side by side under the clear ticklish flow.

"Do it. You'll like it, I promise."

Margaret starts taking off her shoes. Robby stands, hands in pockets, hesitating.

"I don't want to get wet."

The image of the three of them sitting in a row with bare feet dipped in water for no apparent reason is a ridiculous one. Robby frowns at the thought.

Margaret steps into the water and emits a shriek. She walks up and down awkwardly, her toes grasping on to the slippery stones, shoes in hand.

"Okay, then," says Robby as though compelled, and removes his shoes. He plunges his feet in, standing across from his mother.

"So you came here when you were a kid?"

"I spent hours gazing down, splashing, picking up stones and placing them back down into the water, daydreaming . . . You know why I love it here? In the city time is flat, you know, dictated by events and clocks. It's part of the order of things; whereas, here, when you sit with your feet in the stream and look at the stones, what is time? How long it takes for the flow of water to make the stones perfectly smooth? How long it takes for the fallen branch to rot, or for the rays of the sun to soak the leaves of that birch over there, or for your feet to get really cold? To speak of 10:30 or 7:15 is meaningless. Animals awaken when they do, farmers are up with their roosters, the brook never sleeps and the moss keeps gathering . . . "

Robby looks at Margaret as their mother stops speaking.

"Mom?" Margaret says now. "Mom, can I live here with you? We can get some chickens, plant things, like tomatoes . . . I don't know . . . or flowers, and sell them in the market."

"Hmm, that's an idea. Maybe, a small garden just for us this summer . . . "

She looks up at Robby standing in the middle of the brook, hands on hips, his face turned up to the sky, looking at tree tops and clouds in the fading afternoon glimmer, golden light falling like so many leaves on the water around him, his head a ball of fire behind his childish face, the image of a man-boy from ancient times flickering over his young awkward stance. It is gone by the time he dangles his arms down.

"Come here," Selma waves at them. "Come here fast!"

They walk towards her slowly through the bubbling waters. She grabs them by their waists for a hug, inhaling the smell of them.

"Help me get up will you?"

They pull her up by the arms dutifully, unaware of her secret motive: the sudden burst of affection that needed their touch.

❧

At that precise moment, Thomas has finished chewing the last morsel of chicken on his plate at the Ritz in Montreal, and as it slides softly down his throat, the last molar on the left side declares its presence with a sharp pain boring through his lower jaw.

His business associates watch him hold the side of his face with a grimace.

"What's wrong?" exclaims one with a French accent.

"My tooth," Thomas manages to mumble. The men around him look concerned.

"There is a medical building filled with dentists around the block from here, I can take you now if you like," one of the associates offers, rising from his blue velvet-covered chair.

Thomas nods weakly, the grimace tight on his face. "So sorry," he mumbles again, looking around the table at the concerned faces.

They quickly rise as a younger associate leads Thomas towards the door and helps him into his coat, before sitting back down.

❧

Waiting for the dentist to see him, Thomas sits on an old mustard-coloured couch beside a seventy-year-old platinum blonde who smells of mothballs. He leans forward to ease the pain, catching as he does, a glimpse of September walking down the corridor holding a tray of utensils, her white mask hanging around her neck. Fresh lemon-coloured uniform, semi-opaque so he can see her camisole through the fabric. Her chestnut hair is pulled back into a ponytail that swings as she hurries along. He momentarily forgets the pain as his eyes follow her until she disappears through a closed door. The platinum blonde is absorbed in her glossy magazine. The wind outside swells the curtains like sails over the half-open window of the waiting room. Overcast skies. Pain shoots through the tooth once more, making him wince, hand on cheek.

⁀

"Sir?"

He looks up. The assistant in the lemon-coloured uniform and latex gloves ushers him to the dental chair.

"The dentist will be right with you," she says with polite efficiency and turns her back to check the instruments gleaming in the neon glare of the room.

"I appreciate his seeing me like this. One moment I was chewing my food, and the next I felt like a knife went through my brain," he says, trying to smile.

"Sounds bad. You're from out of town?"

"Yes, on business."

"Have you done any sightseeing yet?"

"Do highways and office buildings count?"

She smiles, looking at the information sheet. "Mr Be . . . "

"Call me Thomas," he waves. "It's hard to pronounce, even for me."

She moves the x-ray arm close to his cheek, and proceeds to take the x-ray, moving fluidly.

"What is your name, then?" he asks.

The dentist enters. A white-haired man with hairy forearms and a golden wrist watch, a creaseless white jacket and pink hands puffy from constant washing.

"So, what have we here, Mr . . . " he peeks at the long name on the chart.

"Call me Thomas, please," Thomas says and starts telling the story of his tooth.

The man in the white hair and coat pokes around his teeth with his mirror and hook.

"Many large fillings. Sometimes the tooth continues rotting underneath." He hits a few teeth with his mirror, pulls the lower lip down with his pink index finger. "You should change those fillings some day." He hits again and Thomas's feet jerk as he moans.

"Aha!" says the dentist, "that's the one." He knocks it again with his mirror. Thomas moves in his seat, trying not to scream, wondering why he hit him again.

"Indeed," says the white-haired dentist. "Better make sure before digging. You may need a root canal, you know. The nerve may be infected. Sometimes air travel triggers this process. I understand you flew in not long ago?"

"A couple of days," Thomas attempts to say.

September glides in, lemon-fabric, fresh air and a whiff of citric perfume with swinging hair all at once, holding the x-ray. She smiles at Thomas before handing it to the dentist.

Thomas smiles back wondering how old she is.

"Mr Thomas," the dentist says, "I will have to do a nerve block, now. Please open wide."

Thomas opens his eye to see the needle twinkling in front of his face. A shudder goes through him. *When did he get it ready? I wasn't paying attention.* He feels the cheek being separated from the gums by the dentist's finger then the sting and slowly spreading paralysis. His cheeks, gums, tongue move in his mouth like foreign objects. His enlarged and puffy lips hang inanimately, like meat in a supermarket, cut off from their life supply. It gives him a feeling of stupidity, the freezing, which he knows he'll take with him when he leaves the clinic. He imagines death being a feeling akin to this, where consciousness is permanently frozen, along with the lips, legs, and heart.

When the dentist is finished drilling, pasting, and filling, Thomas has his bib taken off by the lemon-themed woman with the swinging ponytail. He is offered tissue to wipe his foreign lips, which he has difficulty locating on his face without the help of a mirror. *I must be drooling.* Embarrassment rises within him as he dabs half his face liberally. He never managed to get the assistant's name, he realizes with dismay. *She is probably married, anyway, or has someone.* He reasons this as he pulls out his business card, and writes the name of his hotel, his room number behind it. He does not want to risk drooling by asking her the question, so he proceeds to write it down, "Would you have supper with me tonight?" He hands it to her in the waiting room as the receptionist prepares an invoice.

"Thank you. I'm sorry, no," she responds curtly.

He puts his finger up to stop her from going away. He takes the invoice handed to him and writes behind it, "Have you had lunch?" September smiles, "No."

He hides his mouth with his hand. "Then, let me take you out for lunch?"

"You can't eat," she continues smiling as she leads him towards the waiting room and away from the receptionist's curious ears.

"But you can!" He tries again hiding his mouth. "Besides, it'll cheer me up."

"There is a restaurant right around the corner. I only get half an hour's break or so. Is that okay?"

"Sure."

"Wait for me downstairs, then, I'll be a minute," she says in a low voice, making sure the receptionist cannot decipher her words.

e∿

September meets Thomas at the entrance of the neo-classical-looking medical building from the turn of the nineteenth century. Golden laurel wreaths trim the tall ceilings at the edges. He is admiring the carton-pierre when she saunters up beside him, her uniform hidden under a thick jacket.

"I'm ready," she says, "and thanks again."

"My pleasure," he manages. "You will do all the talking, I hope. I cannot feel my lips."

"Why are you taking me out for lunch?" she asks.

"Between you and the businessmen waiting at the Ritz, I figure your company will be more cheerful. It was a tough choice, though."

She grins.

"Before we get to the restaurant, let me make something clear. I don't mind making your acquaintance during lunch, but don't get sleazy and sticky with me. I don't like sleazy men."

"Me neither," he replies quickly, "I never go out with sleazy men, myself."

She giggles. "Also, I can't stand married men on business trips who try to get laid at any cost. Are you married?"

"Separated." There is a tinge of guilt in his voice.

"Well, I'm not available and you're out of luck." She stops short. "Still want to do lunch?" A cloud of cold air surrounds her mouth.

"My goodness, Canadian women are tough, aren't they?"

"I don't have any use for people who waste my time."

"Guys must try to pick you up from that dental chair on a daily basis."

She points at the diner across the street. "Not much of a place, but the service is fast. I don't get much time for lunch," she apologizes.

They sit on ruby-coloured vinyl bench seats, the Formica table between them. A woman with a pink uniform and white apron comes by with her notepad, saying "Hi honey, how's it going?" She pats September on the shoulder. "So what's it going to be? Today's special is pepper steak and mashed potatoes."

"Do you know what you'll have?" Thomas asks September, hiding his mouth with his hand.

"I'll have the special," she replies.

"And what about the gentleman?"

"A glass of water, I guess."

"He can't eat. Frozen," explains September to the waitress. "Thanks, Daisy!"

Daisy walks away in her rubbery white running shoes.

"So Daisy's your friend?" he leans toward September.

"No, I eat here often. We know each other. I'm September, by the way."

"Nice to meet you. Were you born in September?"

"No," she smiles.

"So why September?"

"Guess my mother liked it . . . "

"I see," he nods, not seeing at all. He observes her from across the table, the chestnut hair pulled away from her pale forehead. The eyebrows not very carefully plucked, the full well-chiselled lips, the slightly long nose. She will only give what she wants when she wants to. It is this unspoken statement her body makes with each gesture and gaze which probably attracts all these unwanted dental chair suitors, he figures.

"So, what's there to do in Montreal when one isn't working?"

"Depends on what you like . . . Eating is always a good idea; the food in Montreal is generally quite good . . . Except here . . . If you like dancing, there are a few clubs, quite a few places if you like playing pool, having a drink . . . That sort of thing. Old Montreal, etc. You should check out a tourist guide or something." She quickly cuts a morsel of her pepper steak and hides it in her mouth. She chews mechanically and swallows, before adding, "Walking's always easy, downtown."

"Are you from the suburbs?" he asks.

"No. I live in the centre."

"My hotel is beside the airport, and there isn't much to do around there, I noticed . . . "

"Why stay there?"

"Efficiency. I'm only staying a few days, all my meetings are in offices around that area. When you travel as much as I do, cities begin to blend into one another and they no longer matter. You simply yearn to be home, in your own bed."

"If that's the case, why are you asking me about what to do in this one?"

"I figured I'd stay downtown for tonight, be close to your dentist, in case I need to go back to him tomorrow morning. Perhaps later you'd like to show me the Montreal you like?"

"I'm going back to work. I said I wasn't available for anything later. I thought you heard."

"You're married, no doubt. I apologize for insisting." He doesn't want to seem sleazy. "So this work you do, the dental thing, did you go to school for it?"

"No."

She takes another bite and chews quickly. As soon as she swallows, she explains, "I studied anthropology."

"Oh? And so, why this?"

"I needed a job. Couldn't find anything else. Had to pay the rent. I have a kid."

He nods, understanding. "I have two. Teenagers."

She looks up from her steak quickly. He says, "I won't show you pictures. You thought I'd do that, didn't you?"

"Most people do. I'm almost finished. I'll have to go back in a few more minutes. This was very nice of you, Mr Thomas."

"Just Thomas. Sounds odd, the way you say it."

"I wouldn't mind a coffee. You can probably have one too."

He orders two coffees from Daisy who brings the pot and pours a partly transparent brown liquid into two thick, rustic-looking white cups. He waits for Daisy to leave.

"This doesn't look like coffee . . . " he whispers.

"Taste it." She smiles, her eyes lighting up with mischief. "It'll grow on you."

He takes a tentative sip. "No, it won't," he says, pushing his cup away.

She takes a few sips and rises, putting her jacket back on. She extends her hand, which he shakes.

"What time does the clinic open in the morning?" he asks as she moves away.

"8:30 AM." She rushes out, leaving a hint of citrus in the air.

❧

That night September dreams of Salvador and Thomas sitting in the dental chair, their faces confused into one person, smiling and gaunt in turn. She struggles with vague feelings of guilt, elation and hope without being able to name or separate them. After a long tiresome sleep, she awakens, confused and irritable. She dresses her son and out they go into the cool morning air, the bare tree branches above their heads still waiting for the right moment to shoot thousands of spring buds out at once.

"How do they know when it is time to bloom?" asks Eric as he rushes to keep up beside her.

"Who's they?" she asks absentmindedly.

"The trees."

"Sunlight I guess, and warmer weather . . . "

"What about sunlight?"

"The angle at which the sun's rays hit the earth changes, because of the way the world turns around the sun. It's tilted. I'll show you later, with a ball and your flashlight. Less of a slant means it's spring and the trees get more light and buds form on the branches."

❧

They reach Carré St Louis where Leonard is walking one of his Great Danes around the water fountain, holding his coffee mug, from which hot brown liquid spills in small jolts onto his coat sleeve every time the large dog moves away. September looks down as she continues walking, hoping Leonard will not notice them. He does. He pulls the unwilling animal sideways, spilling more coffee on the already stained left cuff, to get closer to September, who continues along, having now looked up, and with a quick dismissive wave of her free hand hopes to make him understand she is in a hurry and will not stop to converse. She walks faster, pulling the boy along as he tries to adjust his small steps to her large strides. Her heels strike the pavement with a "toc poc, toc poc, tocpoc tocpoc" rhythm that Eric finds amusing as he lets himself be pulled across the street and down into the subway.

"Why do cats poop in a box and dogs go anywhere?"

"I have no idea . . . "

"Maybe cats hide their poop so dogs won't know where they are. Because they're scared of dogs. Dogs don't care; they're not afraid of cats." He finishes his sentence, his wide-open eyes still following his thought.

"Interesting idea. Well," she says, holding onto the escalator hand bar, "then why do we flush our poop down toilets? Are we, too, afraid of dogs?"

A man passing beside them with his briefcase glances quickly at her as she speaks.

"No, we're not afraid. Our poop stinks more. That's why we have to get rid of it."

"Nice morning chat we're having in the metro!"

He laughs, holding his head back. September looks at her child looking jolly and forgets her irritation. She gives him a kiss.

When she enters the dental office, the receptionist rises, smiling, and points at a gigantic bouquet of yellow flowers inside cellophane wrappings.

"For you," she whispers unable to contain her curiosity. "There is a card right here!" She points, her hand fluttering about the flowers. September opens the small envelope.

"Thank you." It says simply.

"Secret admirer," she nods.

"Oooh!" claps the receptionist. "This is so exciting!"

"Would you like to take them home?" September asks, looking mildly amused by the woman's agitation.

"Oh, no. They're for you. Is it the businessman who was here with the toothache? I thought he was rather good looking . . . "

"Really? I hadn't paid attention." September goes off to the washroom to change into her uniform.

"He looked well-off, too," the receptionist says to herself.

e⁓

As September goes through her busy morning, she does not even once suppose that Thomas might be sitting at the greasy spoon down the street, having sips of the insipid coffee in one of their thick white porcelain cups, waiting for her to break for lunch and enter the small restaurant. And she does, in her usual abrupt way, holding the two sides of her jacket together over her unbuttoned uniform. Her purse swings down from her shoulder as she turns and waves at Daisy, who makes eyes at her. She follows the eyes and finds Thomas sitting at the far corner of the restaurant sipping coffee and looking at her. There is a jolt between her ribs and inexplicably a trembling deep in her chest, seeing the grey-haired man with his sharp blue eyes waiting for her. He does not smile, nor does he get up; he simply continues to gaze at her until she approaches the table. Once she arrives, he rises and walks around the table to remove her coat and pull out her chair.

They sit. She puts her hands under the table.

"Thank you for the flowers," she says. "I'm not sure why you sent them, or why you even thanked me. It was really not necessary."

"No, it wasn't. I wanted to please you. Did I?"

"Look, I'm sorry if this sounds rude, but to me you're some random guy in a nice suit. Tomorrow you'll catch your plane and that will be it. I mean, what do you want from me?"

"Nothing in particular. I enjoyed your company. I wanted to enjoy it again. There isn't much else. Tomorrow I'll catch my plane. Today I'm here having lunch with you. Can you not have lunch with a random guy in a suit on a random day of your life?"

"The flowers, they were all yellow."

"You had a citrus thing about you yesterday, the perfume, the uniform, even the camisole, I think. I thought maybe yellow was a good colour. It seemed so."

"You saw my camisole?"

"That yellow uniform is transparent. Isn't that why you wear a camisole?"

"Whatever," she waves her hand, annoyed. "If you don't mind, I have to order lunch, the clock is ticking."

"I've ordered it. The special, I figured. Spaghetti and meatballs. Here it is."

Daisy has brought two plates heaped with orange-looking spaghetti with a few meatballs sitting atop the pile.

"Enjoy your meal," says Daisy as she goes away.

"I don't always order the special. This stuff doesn't look good," September says, sniffing it.

"Think of your childhood. There were meals you weren't inclined to eat, but did it anyway . . . You did have a childhood, didn't you?"

"Very funny. You start first. If you don't drop dead, I'll eat too. This reminds me of cafeteria food."

"Oh, yes. I grew up with it. Boarding school, most of my youth. You?"

"No. Why were you in a boarding school?"

"Builds character."

"It does?"

He shrugs. "My father was a jerk. He never kissed me or ruffled my hair even. He didn't want me growing up 'glued to my mother's skirts.' I don't even remember my mother's skirts, come to think of it. You know, you had to become a man by the age of ten. That sort of thing . . . " He sticks his fork into the orange mound and begins to twist it. "This is how I see it. When you grow up poor, you don't get much of a childhood. When you grow up rich, same thing. Forget childhood. When you're somewhere in the middle, not dreary, not flashy, childhood happens . . . It's not a theory or anything. Just an observation. I'm probably wrong . . . " He looks up.

"So you didn't have a proper childhood?"

"I don't know . . . When you think of childhood, you tend not to think of day in and out, play with the red truck, run after your friends, eat gruel. Your childhood comes to you like a raft, right, floating on something shapeless and fluid . . . a memory pond. No? It isn't about instances, it's about the drift, the colours associated with it, the sounds, the insides of things. Do you know what I mean?"

"Are you really a businessman?"

"I wonder about that too. I've been in an odd state of mind for the last little while. My wife and I, when we separated, it seemed like the wrong thing had happened. I was devastated. It still felt that way until I got to the dentist. We had the life everyone envied, we rarely fought, it was good, in a way. In fact, a lot of what we call 'good' is actually 'dull' it seems to me, now. Yes, we had the day-to-day thing, but there was no raft floating through the memory pond, ever. I sat in that waiting room, doubled in pain and saw you pass by. The yellow transparency, the camisole sliding over your figure, the lemony perfume, the swinging ponytail. Beside me was the open window, and the curtain puffing up like a sail. It all made sense. Maybe I'm delirious? What did your dentist give me anyway? Am I drugged out of my brains?"

"Painkillers will do that to you," she says, sticking her fork into the spaghetti.

"I probably won't ever see you again, I figure. This disturbs me. Yet I don't know the first thing about you . . . Well, you don't like spaghetti and meatballs, I guess I know that. You passed me by like fresh lemonade and I want to dump my entire life to start over. This is crazy . . . "

"Can I tell you a secret? This uniform I wear is embarrassing to me . . . It reminds me daily of what isn't. It represents everything that isn't."

"Run away with me. We'll frame the uniform. It'll be a relic for me to worship."

She swallows her forkful. "Are you nuts, or is this a joke?"

He leans back from his plate. "Which part? The relic or the running away?"

She leans towards him with a frown, "You're a guy with a toothache who's leaving tomorrow. You live . . . I don't even know . . . where again?"

"Greece."

"Right; you have two kids and are separated. You're speaking non-sense over a dish of horrendous pasta . . . Daisy?" she turns and calls the waitress.

Daisy rushes towards them from the other side of the narrow restaurant. September points to the pasta. "This isn't working for me. I think it's making the gentleman delirious. Did the cook lose his Valium in it?"

Daisy leans towards them with eyes wide open and whispers, "Never order the Thursday special." She straightens up and continues in a normal voice, "Do you want something else, hon?"

"Something real quick, please, Daisy. I only have thirteen minutes left."

"Salad?"

"Okay."

"The gentleman?"

"He'll have salad too."

Daisy rushes away with the mounds of spaghetti. Thomas sighs.

"I only have thirteen minutes left in my life to convince you I'm not a lunatic. Look, please meet me after work. An hour. I spotted a bistro around the corner. They have small round tables and nice music. We can have a glass of wine. Don't say no. Please."

"I don't know if I can make arrangements. Give me your hotel number, I'll call you later."

She stabs at clumps of bland iceberg lettuce and fills her mouth before getting up.

"Sorry, I have to go."

He hands her the paper napkin with the hotel name and his room number.

"Don't know the phone number," he says.

"I'll find it. I'll call you around six or so."

e⌒

September spends the afternoon in a daze, handing instruments to the dentist, nodding when spoken to, occasionally glancing at the bouquet of yellow flowers in the waiting room. Between patients she calls her neighbour Carina to see if she can stay with Eric while she meets Thomas. Carina agrees. She then finds the hotel telephone number and calls Thomas to tell him she will meet him at seven at the reception. She does all this without thinking, lest she change her mind.

She picks up her son from daycare, rushes home to shower and change. She settles on the red dress, the black tights and the pointy black boots after some deliberation. The doorbell rings, offering Carina with her guitar. Eric is delighted. September leaves.

At the hotel reception, she does not see him at first. There is a crowd of tourists checking in, some of them sitting at tables and armchairs waiting. She stands by the entrance looking around; faces enter and leave her vision, bodies, feet, hands, moving in haphazard choreography, up and down stairs, stepping into elevators, leaving through revolving doors. For a few moments she stands there, feeling awkward, wondering if she's caught up in a meaningless pursuit. His hand touches her shoulder. She turns to meet him. His lips curve into a smile. She sees the blue of his eyes and the glimmer of his grey hair in the light of the large chandeliers.

He holds her hands sandwiched between his warm palms. "I'm so happy to see you."

"I'm glad to see you too," she says, meaning it to sound formal; but it comes out genuine and slightly nervous.

As they walk outside, he turns to her and says, "This is the first time in my life I don't know where I'm going . . . And what I'm doing!" His chuckle is short. "I'm the sort who always has a plan, who organizes things to death. Really. Since yesterday, I have no idea." He stuffs his hands into his pockets. "This is not a sexy thing for a guy to admit on a first date, is it? I don't think I can find that bistro I was telling you about in the dark."

They turn onto Ste-Catherine Street.

"There is always a crowd on this street. Why? There aren't even that many restaurants or bars that I can see."

September smiles. "I know. It's mysterious, isn't it? The first rays of sunlight hit the pavements in the spring, and at the first whiff of thawed ice and dog poop, the whole city is here on Ste-Catherine, walking back and forth, cars cluttering the narrow street. It's a collective thing . . . I've grown up here and always wondered. Now you come from far away, a stranger, and make a similar observation. Odd, huh?"

"Many see the same things, few wonder the same way about them. Maybe that's the basis of all great friendships?"

"To wonder about the same things?"

"To be struck, yes, by congruent thoughts, or feelings, maybe . . . "

"What happened with your wife? Maybe this is inappropriate, sorry . . . Forget it."

"Better to forget it, yes."

A chill descends as they walk around a corner in search of a restaurant. September thinks she should find one quickly on account of her aching feet in high heels.

"Here's one," she points at a Mexican restaurant with strains of cheerful Latin music spilling out from the door every time people go in.

As they settle and choose from the menu, he blurts out, "I had affairs."

She puts her glass down.

He continues, "I was a serial cheater," and opens the large linen napkin. "She knew. She always knew."

September takes another sip of water.

"Look at me, I have a couple of hours to make a good impression on you, and I mess it up."

"You're the guy who's taking a plane in the morning. No worries. Life will continue as before, tomorrow." She winks with a good-natured smile.

"You mean you're not running away with me? You mean, you'll do that citrus thing for a thousand other men?"

"I'm afraid so," she laughs.

"Then I won't take my plane."

"Empty threats!"

"What's a guy to do? So you have a little boy, do you?"

"Hmm. I do."

"And his father? He's not around."

"Whatever gave you that idea?"

"No citrus thing for him then, huh?"

"No, I save it for strangers with rotten teeth."

"So, is there any way of knowing more about you, other than 'no spaghetti and meatballs'?"

"It's a bit pointless, isn't it? My telling you about my past catastrophes, your telling me about your wrecks . . . Then what?"

"What do two strangers who aren't so strange to each other talk about? You want to do the weather report? By the way, is this some sort of Canadian obsession? These business partners of mine, they can spend a good half hour on temperature issues. I thought this was an icebreaker, the first day. But every day? Then I go buy gum in a store, 'dépanneur' you call it, right? I get another weather report there. I bet if we start chatting up the waiter, he'll also give us the dirty on today's weather. What's it with you people?"

September bursts into laughter.

"We respect our weather . . . It can kill you. You've got to know what's going on."

"I like the way you laugh," he smiles, joining his hands into a pyramid above his plate. "I don't want to leave Montreal yet."

"Anybody waiting for you in Greece?"

"No. I have to pick up my kids on the way. They're on spring break at their mother's in Sweden."

"International family?"

"Hmm. It gets complicated. We're trying to figure out what is best for them, Sweden or wherever I am. I travel a lot; my wife, ex-wife, does-n't have business trips. But the kids, they have friends in Greece; it's kind of hard for them to go to a new school now. I really don't know what's best. Plus, they have spent most of their time with her, I haven't been around much. I sense they feel strange around me."

"And why Greece?"

"My business took me there. It took me many places. The kids have gone to school all over the world, practically."

"So they probably won't mind moving to Sweden."

"Who knows . . . Anyone waiting for you at home?"

"My son."

"No husband, boyfriend?"

"Not really. I've recently been . . . disengaged."

"So, any plans for the rest of your life?"

"I'm thinking of taking up knitting."

"Many mittens and hats in your kid's future."

She smiles. "What about the rest of yours, then?"

"I fall madly in love with a beautiful woman who smells of lemonade. I drop everything and spend my days in Montreal, getting my teeth fixed, wearing mittens and scarves."

"Are you trying to get into my pants?" She throws her head back for a throaty laugh.

"You're not wearing any; if you were, I'd probably be thinking of it."

She takes a sip of wine, looks around, averts his gaze.

"Do you want to hear a more serious answer about the rest of my life?" She asks this after another quick sip.

He leans over the table, ready to listen.

"I was walking down my street last summer. It was one of those glorious days, the sun shining, bright green leaves on the trees, the whole world out in the streets, sitting in outdoor cafés, kites flying in the sky. There was a couple in their front yard, watering their plants with a hose. They were laughing and hosing each other down, running around the tiny yard. It was the picture of all that has eluded me, somehow. I wanted to stand there and stare. I couldn't, of course, so I kept walking on, glancing back at them, so completely oblivious to everything but their play. I got home and shut the door behind me. My apartment is dark even on the sunniest days . . . I wept. Anyway, that's it."

Thomas nods, looking at the oval face, the sudden spring of melancholy in the hazel eyes, the small smile showing the thinnest sliver of ivory between her lips, hazelnut hair falling like unfinished snakes on her shoulders. He wants to reach over and caress the top of her left hand lying on the white tablecloth and tell her he wishes to give it all to her: the tiny yard, the sunny morning, the cracks in the concrete sidewalk from which dandelions spring, the water drops that cause giggles and everlasting happiness as they slide down a wet face on a hot day. He wants to stand up and promise these to her, realizing for the first time this may be the only promise worth making, as a man to a woman. His heart accelerates, thudding into his ears so he cannot hear himself speak. He sees her right hand letting go of the fork and hiding under the table to be met by her left hand lying softly on the table seconds ago, the image of exposed tender sadness running for cover.

" . . . dedicate my life to giving you these things," he hears himself say.

"Thomas," her voice comes out soft and blurred, "don't try to fix a stranger's life in one evening. You can't."

"September, look at me. Middle-aged man, 53. I have lived like some prick all my life. Yes, yes. Listen. A runaway life, going through the motions. Acquiring money, status, wife, acquiring everything. My father's unquestioned tradition. My wife used to say my universe was a greased machine and everyone around me I used as gears. It came out in arguments mostly and I brushed it off as the meanness of a frustrated wife. I reduced her to that. I saw to it that she had the best of everything, locked up in my stuffy universe while I went around sleeping with . . . other frustrated women who envied her because she was rich and pampered. It's all very pathetic really. When a machine like mine crashes, what is left? A few screws, a few gears . . . scattered debris. A prick in the midst of it looking forward to eternal stiffness. Pardon the pun, it wasn't voluntary."

He takes a deep breath and loosens his tie, pulling it sideways as he continues, "I know what you'll say . . . "

"No, you don't."

"Yes, I can imagine. Now that you've understood where you went wrong, go ask her for another chance. No. There are old habits there, and not enough inspiration."

"I wasn't going to say that."

He stops pulling at his tie, looks at her.

"I wasn't going to say anything. Why don't you take that tie off?"

"I should," he mumbles and removes the tie and shoves it into his pocket.

"You don't strike me as a prick at all. Maybe you were stuck. It happens all the time, to all sorts of people."

"Tell me now, who loves you?" He tears a piece of bread and throws it between his teeth.

She chuckles, "Everybody!"

"I'm sure. Just look at me, I crossed an ocean for one date with you."

She rolls her eyes.

"Why else am I here?" He volleys another small piece of bread into his mouth.

"For some business meetings."

"No. That was the excuse. The aching tooth took me to you."

"You're odd."

"You never answered my question."

She looks at him, not understanding.

"Who loves you?"

"My son, I hope. My friends. There is a man also. He loves me, but . . . "

"He's a fool. Your mother?"

"I was adopted. My adoptive mother died. My biological mother I never met. I like to think she loved me enough to give me away. Who knows? I make up scenarios where she became brain-dead due to an accident, and was pregnant, etc. There is a whole range from the accidental to the sordid that I have considered over the years. But I did have a mother who cared for me in the end, and that is what truly counts, no? Not necessarily who has loved you, but how much you've been loved and how much of it you can give away, pass on or whatever it is we do with love. Maybe I'm wrong . . . " She looks away, becomes thoughtful.

He leans back, moving the clean knife back and forth on the tablecloth.

She continues, "Do you ever wonder about love, the soul, these things . . . where do they actually happen? What are they? When people pass away, what happens to their love, and to the love we feel for them? Their memories and thoughts? Do they just vanish? Or are they things that remain in between? Someone once told me that any and every sound uttered stays in the air, or leaves a signature of sorts. If one day they find a way to process these sounds, all the voices and noises in all the history of humankind will still be there, waiting. Anyway, I'm babbling. Sorry."

She cuts a piece of her food mechanically and puts it in her mouth, not looking up.

"Where I grew up," he says after clearing his throat, "reading coffee cups is common. Some readers are so good they can tell you the main events of your future life while you're still young. Of course, when you listen to them, it sounds like total nonsense. They may say 'I see a door', and then describe in exact detail the knocker on it. Then, perhaps, the people living behind that door, or what your connection is to that door. Or not. Then they go on to another detail, they may give you a name, a date, intervals of time, a physical or moral description of a person. It almost sounds like a bad dream you get from indigestion. You shrug it off and forget about it. Years or months or even hours later, something happens, and you recognize the door with the knocker. You realize that this precise event or object already existed somewhere, at least in the reader's mind, but you weren't aware of it. It's always been an odd, uncomfortable thought for me. Where did this event exist before it happened? Is life a sort of reverse cosmic echo where everything already exists in anticipation of its occurrence?"

℮

Not far from Carré St-Louis, Salvador is preparing his suitcase in John's apartment. He is free to leave the city, having been cleared of suspicion in the death of his wife. The light is muted from the 45-watt bulbs darkened by age and dust. He folds a navy blue cardigan whose third button is about to come loose. He thinks about looking for a needle and thread to tighten it, hesitating before shaping the thick knitwear into a bulky square. The button will slip off unexpectedly, he thinks, the cardigan will start looking shabby and he will forget it in a drawer, never to wear it. As he places it in the suitcase, he knows that its fate is already sealed. He wonders when all the clothes Claire bought for him will finally meet this same fate. Will she remain with him until the last pair of briefs have thinned out? He realizes that he does not want to leave, Halifax seems a cold distant city to his strange heart. He puts a few more items in the suitcase. It is not so much where he will go as the fact that he must do so, having already publicly uttered his intention. Like the cardigan, he muses, falling apart but packed to go. He looks up from his suitcase to find Claire sitting in John's faded armchair, the way she used to look before losing her battle. Blond and blue, legs crossed, grey skirt crumpled above the thighs, a high-heeled shoe slightly dangling off her narrow foot, an ironic, mocking smile curving her lips.

"Claire!" He croaks.

She looks at him and nods, "Bon voyage, chéri. I came to say goodbye."

She uncrosses her legs, rises from the chair and walks towards him, her unsteady high heels digging into the plush carpet. She reaches over and touches his arm, gets close to his face. He feels the warm breath of life from her mouth, her manicured nails digging into his arm. The hair on his back stands on edge, hurting his skin. His tongue slowly comes untied in his mouth, and he utters, "Claire, don't. I can't . . . I can't."

He leaps away from her, his heart thudding inside him. She gazes at him for a moment before turning her back; he hears her whisper something as she walks towards the doorway and disappears.

Salvador's torso feels leaden where he remains on the floor, hugging his knees. He hears the sudden brakes of a car, the impatient sound of a honk, someone yelling in the street. The water resumes dripping monotonously in the kitchen sink, the heating pipes make a loud rattle. Then all the audible movements around him stop as suddenly as they began, engulfing the dimly lit room in stark silence. *Halifax, on the other hand,* the thought begins to take shape in the quietude of his mind, *has fog horns.* He goes on to imagine the grey expanse of the ocean, the wetness that fills the air with a scent of iodine, ships slipping through the fog blowing their loud plaintive horns as they arrive in the harbour. This thought raises him from the corner where he sat crouched moments ago fearing his wife's ghost. He steadies his trembling hands on the suitcase, imagining that unknown port, the city streets and lighthouses, the smell of fish. As his mind meanders through imagined roads with unknown names to find the building where a new job awaits him, he is almost convinced life will be kinder to him there. Montreal will fade in his memory to become a place where he once lived, his wife's blood-streaked and lifeless face will recede with it, setting him free of that couch in his apartment, its particular smells and despair, the sight of her ankles wobbling on high heels those drunk nights when he just lay in the darkness of their room anticipating the nauseating smells of liquor and tobacco and perfume ahead of her awkward entrance. Memories will depart, the unhappy years of his life will seem foreign. He imagines pouring them out into the Atlantic Ocean, bucket by bucket on warm starry nights when the current is strong. He gazes while they travel through the water, pass by silent fish, monumental whales, and shipwrecks, and reach some further shore, perhaps even his birthplace. There may be a child skipping stones there, just as he did many decades ago.

September will recede along with his wife's memory. He considers this while carrying his suits and ties to pack into the suitcase. A deep ache begins to slip down the middle of his chest into his stomach at the thought of her. Once it reaches the bottom of his gut, another ache starts to roll down his chest, making his ribcage hurt. He wants to stop packing and run across the street to the yellow door, knock and ask her to go with him, to follow him there with her son, a new life for the three of them. He cannot see it yet, he cannot imagine it, but he wants to and thinks he may, if he tries a little harder, if he focuses as he should. He gets up and starts walking towards the door. A car stops across the street, the lights flickering through the small window beside the door. He peeks out through the blinds and sees September leaving a taxi. There is a man sitting in the back, a man with grey hair who gets out of the car after her and pauses for a moment to speak to the driver. The driver keeps the motor running as the grey-haired man walks September to the door. They speak for a moment as she searches for her keys. He sees them in the partial darkness of the street, silhouettes illuminated by the taxi's lights. They lean towards each other. Salvador remains stuck to the window, wanting to leave but unable to budge. The man raises his arms to hold September by the shoulders. He moves closer to her as she turns towards the door and slightly away from him. The man hugs her and rushes for the taxi without looking back.

Salvador remains pensive, standing by the window long after the babysitter has slipped out through the yellow door. The exterior lights have been turned off and the door is now a greyish shadow illuminated by the slanted light of the lamppost a few feet away.

～

Inside his taxi cab, Thomas sticks his hand into the pocket of his jacket to remove his tie. He caresses the smooth fabric between his fingertips wondering how it is that something so soft to touch can be so suffocating. It is a beautiful tie, with golden diagonal stripes; distinguished, elegant. The taxi drives through an empty avenue he thinks he recognizes.

"Sir," he says, "would you like to have a nice tie?"

"Pardon?" says the driver, looking through the rear-view mirror.

"Do you ever wear ties?"

The man looks in the mirror again, trying to understand the question.

"Sometimes."

"Job interviews?"

"Yes," replies the driver, "sometimes."

"Engineer?"

"Hmm," says the driver, "how could you tell?"

Thomas makes a face. "Don't know. Just a wild guess."

"Because I'm brown?"

"Pardon me? I didn't understand?" Thomas frowns, leaning forward to hear better.

"Did you guess I was an engineer because of my skin colour?"

"How are these related?"

"You're not from here, are you?"

"No . . . Why?"

"Forget it. Civil engineer. All those blown up bridges in my country, and here I am, driving a taxi. So, why are you trying to get rid of your tie in the middle of the night?"

"They never seem to fit me right. If you need one it's yours. Feel it." He reaches over and hands the tie to the driver.

"Good enough. Looks expensive," says the driver, smiling. "I've seen many things driving a taxi, but this is a first. Okay I'll take it. You have enough money for your fare, right?"

"You mean I also have to pay?"

The driver glares through the mirror at Thomas. "Are you one of those drunks looking for trouble in the middle of the night?" He pulls over to stop at a street corner. "If you have no money please step out now or I'll call the police."

Thomas starts laughing. "I was joking, man! Keep driving, will you? I need to get some sleep. Come on . . . What, you want me to show you my wallet? Keep going. I'm tired. It was a joke, okay?"

The driver nods, utters a hesitant, "Okay."

"So, what's this you said about being brown and an engineer? I'm intrigued . . ."

"This is Montreal. Say, you're an engineer and you're brown; chances are you'll drive a taxi for the rest of your life. It's a very nice city, I like it, you know, but . . ."

"What if you're a white engineer and from somewhere else, say

Romania?"

"How good is your French? I don't know . . . You're better off in Toronto. Drive a taxi there!" He bursts into laughter. "We can't all be driving taxis in Montreal, can we? Soon you'll need a PhD to do it. Actually, I already know one who's got it. Here we are . . . Your hotel."

Thomas reaches into his pocket for the fare. He enters the warmth of the hotel lobby.

℮

At the same time, farther up on the hill, a young man is wheeled into the hospital emergency room by paramedics. He is pale, unconscious, his heart rate falling, his stringy blond hair is partly hidden by a mask and tubes. There is a commotion around him as he is taken off the stretcher and wheeled beyond the swinging doors. The intake clerk searches his record to find the next of kin. "I have it," she exclaims, "the father's number, in Outremont." She proceeds to dial the phone number on her monitor. The line keeps ringing until finally an answering machine responds. She leaves a brief and precise message asking the man to come to the hospital immediately.

Four floors up, Mrs Liu is sleeping in her bed, her foot still in the sling, and itchy inside the cast. Her daughter has come from Vancouver to visit, bringing Xiao with her. Mrs Liu is dreaming of her grandson with his ruddy cheeks and ink-black hair. She sees him smile mostly, puffing cold mist from his mouth every time he parts his teeth to laugh. She is patient about her itch now. She knows her daughter is there to take care of her and she no longer has to be alone. She even feels grateful for her accident, because it has brought her daughter to her side. On the phone she could never say to Jiang that her loneliness made her fearful, that she saw danger everywhere, and darkness lurking, that she was not at all brave but a tired old woman whose suffering had no words, no windows, no respite. How could she say these things to the baby she had saved? In Vancouver, she thinks, she will walk Xiao to school, make him the dumplings he likes, listen to everyone but herself.

him, puffing his sails. Amazing how easy it is to sail, he thinks, I'm not even doing anything, yet the boat is slipping away from the shore so smoothly. He turns back to look at the beach. Surprisingly, his father is there, clad in a suit, holding a briefcase, waving at him. How ridiculous and small he looks standing at the edge of the lake in his stiff outfit. Is he there to watch me sail? Is he actually there to see me off? Benoit looks around in disbelief, thinking his father may have come to see others, and may in fact be waving at someone else. But there is no one else on the lake. He suddenly realizes there is a shade of desolation to the water; murky colours of death surround his sailboat. I did not pay attention, he panics; if I had, I would have noticed there was no other shore. The wind is strong and the sail taut; his boat slices through the water like a razor, bending to the side. His fingers try to grip onto the side of the boat as it topples over. Water fills his lungs, he gasps for air. I'm drowning. He flaps his hands, hoping his father will swim to his side from the shore. "Sauve-moi, papa," he wants to say, "don't let me perish!" A hand is pulling him up, but he still cannot breathe. He is being pulled up and up and up through the brownish opaque waters of the lake, yet it keeps getting deeper and darker around him. "Come back Benoit, come back," someone says, someone not his father. It is a familiar voice travelling to his ears through the thick water. "Open your eyes Ben, take a deep breath, deep . . . Breathe, boy, breathe!" He tries to breathe again and this time it feels like the water has a pocket of air which he sucks into his hurting lungs. It is excruciating to breathe again. Like knives in the chest. He finds himself on the shore, strange faces converging on him; faces without bodies. He tries to breathe once more, despite the pain. "Ben!" A face comes closer. He's got shiny black hair this one, an aquiline nose, deep-set eyes. I know this face, but how? He tries to open his eyes wider, and as he does, the uniforms attached to the faces come into focus, so do the silhouettes of people standing around him in a greenish room against blinding lights. This is no shore. Where is the lake? He looks around, moving his eyes from side to side. "He is with us!" someone exclaims. From far away he hears a regular beep.

"Where?" he croaks. John comes close to hm and says, "At the hospital. You're safe." Benoit closes his eyes. His lips start moving slowly before the whisper escapes, "Nurse Ratchett . . . "

John chuckles. Benoit does not open his eyes, passes out instead. He misses his father's visit a couple of hours later.

℮

John returns home that morning on the empty bus which takes him along Pine Avenue; he stares out the dusty window at the busy street as it speeds away behind him, his eyes not looking at anything in particular, leaving his mind to focus on Benoit. Perhaps, he thinks, perhaps, I can be a raft for this boy in this random drift. There may be someplace to go, something to do. This being alone, a burden. This not having found . . . Not being needed.

When he gets off, his feet shuffle down the street, past the yellow door shedding its grey cloak in the light of the rising sun. He expects to be greeted by the smell of Salvador's morning coffee when he unlocks his door. Instead, he finds silence, the lingering smell of aftershave.

"Ho! Salvador?" he calls out.

Nothing moves.

He opens the bathroom door, then his closet door and sits on his bed. Salvador is gone.

There is an envelope leaning against the small jade Buddha. He walks up to it, tears it open. Some money. He counts $500. Inside the envelope is another sheet of paper folded in three which he proceeds to unfold and read. Salvador's handwriting is studied and careful, moving along the paper stylishly with top heavy *ts,* and *ys* that flourish at the bottom. After reading the letter, John folds it back and takes it to his packsack, removes the notebook and places it inside. He walks around the apartment aimlessly until he tires of not finding something interesting to do. He takes off his clothes to prepare for sleep.

℮

Mrs Liu, having woken up at dawn and waited impatiently for the sun to rise, is now brushing her white hair back, looking at herself in the mirror. Her daughter and grandson will come to see her this morning. She turns her head to the left to look at the right side of her face in the small mirror. Her eye lingers on her lower cheek sagging down like a pouch. She feels the past with her hand, moves it up and down. *Little Xiao will think me old and ugly.* Sighing, she leans over to the night table and puts down the mirror and brush. She closes her eyes and waits.

Jiang and Xiao come down the corridor to Room 417 hours later to find Mrs Liu sleeping. Jiang walks to the bed and pauses, observing her mother's face. Xiao rushes to the window and sits down on the old arm-chair of faded brown synthetic leather. The radiator beside the chair has silver-coloured coils which he finds fascinating, and he stands up to peek behind. He finds a small cobweb on which he blows mightily and tears it.

"Good morning, mama," exclaims Jiang, leaning over to hug her mother.

Xiao looks at the old woman from the other end of the room.

"Xiao!" calls his grandmother, her face lighting up at his sight. "Come here, my sweet," she waves at the boy.

Xiao approaches the bed, staring at her hanging leg.

"See what your silly grandmother did? She went and got her leg bro-ken. You want to knock on the cast? Go ahead it's hard."

Xiao knocks, and smiles.

"Do you want to write your name there?"

The boy nods and waits for his mother to find a pen in her purse. He signs his name with a flourish under the careful gaze of his grandma.

"Grandma, are you coming to live with us in Vancouver?" he asks in hesitant Cantonese.

"If you want me to, I'll come," she says, beaming, and glances at her daughter.

Her daughter nods. Liu reaches over and holds her daughter's hand, squeezing it. "Thank you, daughter," she says. Jiang smiles and looks away, out the window at the city below.

"I'll make you the best shrimp dumplings you've ever eaten, little

Xiao."

Jiang continues gazing out the window. The clouds are the colour of lead. It might snow again. She remembers snowball fights in Chinatown. Their small apartment above a grocery store that sold ointments and syrups from China, and little dolls and plastic fans. Her mother always busy at her sewing machine by the window upstairs, when she looked up from the street. Mrs Liu was a seamstress, she sewed ladies' clothes, even men's shirts. For a time, everyone had custom-made clothes in Chinatown. As times changed, so did her clientele. She started sewing buttons and hems, making alterations on ready-made clothes, working for dry-cleaning shops around town. "Who paid for your university?" Jiang's husband had asked her once, when she was describing their modest circumstances. "My mother's eyes," she had responded. She grew up wondering about her three sisters left behind in China.

"Mother," she clears her throat, "when you get better, what do you say, we go to China, look for my sisters? Maybe Xiao can come with us too."

Mrs Liu tries to hide her panic. "Little daughter," her voice comes out, plaintive, "this is not a trip for an old woman. You go after I die."

"Mama," Jiang smiles, thinking her mother's refusal has to do with expenses. "It isn't far from Vancouver. Besides, we will stay at nice hotels and everything, we can afford it now. I've been looking for my sisters on the internet. I want to find them. I want you to see them once again. After all these years, and all these sacrifices you've made . . . I want to reunite the family."

Mrs Liu's heart is racing. *Ugly Wu's daughters. My daughters. This is a nightmare.* "Youngest daughter," she says faintly, "the emotion will kill your old mother, surely. Spare me, in these last years of my life. I tell you I won't survive the excitement. You go after I die, with Xiao. Don't take me there. Please."

Jiang looks concerned. "Mother, how can you not want to see your own daughters once more before you die? I don't understand . . . "

"Little daughter, I'm sorry. I just feel so tired and I'm in a lot of pain, inside my bones. We talk of this later, when I'm better. Do you agree?"

Jiang nods, feeling guilty. "You're right, mom. I'm sorry. I just got so excited thinking about the reunion. I always missed my sisters. All my life, I wanted to see their faces, hear their voices. When I was little, in Chinatown, I always thought I would make a lot of money when I grew up and help them. I imagined them crying over there, without you, and felt guilty having you all to myself here in Canada."

"You're a good daughter," smiles Liu, hopeful now that she has averted the danger for a while. "Xiao, tell me, are you smart in school?"

Xiao has gone back to the radiator, looking at the shredded cobweb, wondering where the spider is hiding. He looks at his grandmother momentarily. She used to ask the same question when he was in daycare. *"Are you smart in school?"*

He still does not know how to answer this.

"I don't know."

"Mostly As," says Jiang.

"Good boy," his grandmother nods, satisfied. "You'll become a good accountant."

"No," Xiao shakes his head. "I want to do animation. You know, computer games, things like that. I want to make drawings that move." He does not quite know how to explain this in Cantonese. He looks at his mother for help.

Jiang responds to him in English, "She won't understand. Just agree."

"No," Xiao continues in Cantonese, "not accountant. I want to draw moving pictures."

Mrs Liu frowns, looks at Jiang.

"Is something wrong with the boy's head?"

"He's just a boy, mom . . . He likes to draw."

"You feed him enough fish? When I come, I'll make stewed fish, he'll get smarter."

Jiang speaks to the boy in English, "Next time, just agree. She doesn't understand this stuff. She's old."

Mrs Liu has picked up the last part. She declares in English,

"Grandma old, not stupid."

She is feeling cross now, and her shin hidden by the cast is itchy once again. She looks out the window to see the snow falling thinly over the city, looking like a gauze curtain outside the window.

&

It is almost eleven in the morning when John opens his eyes and looks at the digital clock by his bed. He has been lying fully clothed in bed, eyes closed and mind awake, thinking about Salvador's note, his absence, and the old familiar silence creeping back into his apartment bringing to life the forgotten sounds of dripping faucet, abrupt radiator, and muffled street noises. He rises from his bed and wears his coat hurriedly, leaving the apartment on a sudden impulse. Standing at his doorstep he greets the snow with surprise. There is a thin film of it on the ground. It descends from the sky in small cottony balls. Stealthily, like the paws of a kitten they land, covering all the surfaces with their white silence. He wants to write this observation down before he forgets it. He hurries through the snowfall, towards the café, seeing himself at his favourite wooden table by the window, inhaling the warm aromatic steam of coffee, writing in his notebook while snow falls outside in the park, where squirrels scurry about, their auburn tails like commas undulating through space. And . . . and . . . and . . . after each movement, up the tree, down the trunk, up on the bench, down the leg . . . and . . . and . . . This, he will write. It will be a poem about sitting in a warm café watching squirrels outside as the snow falls in soft, fat, white blotches. Squirrels in Carré St-Louis. He almost runs through the park to the café, lest the thought evaporates, before he reaches for his pen. He feels the exhilaration of having found words; words to match the world he has just discovered. Yes, that's it, he smiles. I am in the world again. Or the world is in me.

As he sits in the café, five minutes later, his hair still wet, he opens the green notebook and writes his thoughts. He writes quickly, scratching out, rewriting, occasionally focusing his eyes intensely onto a spot on the wall, waiting for an image to return. After a while, he sips his coffee.

He flips the pages back until he reaches the beginning of the notebook. He reads forgotten words about remembrance. Although none of the words refer to his childhood, he remembers his childhood being present when he wrote the first paragraph. An ache spreads in his chest. He quickly turns the pages to find something about his imaginary wife and kids, the product of his conversation with Room 415. A few pages forward he finds the poem about Selma's slipper. As he reads it over and over, he can almost smell the red geraniums on the corner of her balcony, the scent of her copper hair on the pillows. The white satin bow on the slipper in the morning sunlight, the sea in front of them. The ferry cutting the harbour in half, silently. Bats zigzagging. That slipper is still with him. It sits at the bottom of the old brown leather suitcase in the small furnace room. He recalls the moment he had rushed downstairs and crossed the street to retrieve it from the sidewalk, his eyes squinting in the sun. He had picked it up and automatically brought it to his nose to breathe in the perfume of her beloved foot. The scent of a woman's pink foot that has been to bed after a shower. The smell of her body concentrated in her heels, as she walks the tiny distances from bathroom to bed, to kitchen to balcony. The smell of caprice. "On a street called Henri-Julien," he starts again and reads the poem once more as he begins to daydream, imagining her in those moments preceding his departure; the vivid colours of her lips and freckles close to his face when she refused to say goodbye. In all those years spent in Montreal, he never once took the slipper out of the suitcase to look at. He thinks about this now, watching the cars carefully drive through the slush on St-Denis. The object itself is merely a dusty remnant. It has the cadaverous look of a thing once imbued with purpose and charm. He shudders at the sudden arrival of death into his thoughts and quickly returns to his last scribbles about a squirrel's tail, snow, and punctuation. He wants to recapture his previous state of elation while rushing through the park, his entire being collapsing around a few words, the almost finding or being found, wanting to reach for the essence of it as he moved through falling snow. And what is *it*? WHAT IS *IT*? He jots down the question and underlines *IT*.

℮⌃

He is once again at work, surrounded by beeps and hushed voices, the smell of iodine and pills.

"Hey John!" waves a nurse as he walks to his locker in the lounge. He goes to the desk, where Anne is reading the newspaper.

"Slow evening, eh?" he greets her.

"I'm not complaining . . . How have you been?"

"Good, good . . . So, your friends from PEI?"

"Yeah, came and left already. His wife is a nurse too. His daughter will soon go to university, maybe McGill, and so on . . . "

"What about him?"

"Same. Greyer, a bit rounder, but same."

"Was it hard?"

"It was okay as long as I didn't look into his eyes, you know, it's the eyes . . . "

He sits down beside her, nodding.

" . . . whenever I looked, something inside me would unravel, you know, and I'd suddenly feel so desperate, like my entire life since I left the island has been . . . " She looks up at the ceiling to regain composure. "Anyway, past is past, right? Nothing to be gained by . . . " She sighs and looks blankly at her newspaper. "Problem is, when you're young, you don't know that some things might never happen to you again. You don't realize that you may never feel . . . "

He nods wisely.

She continues, "Maybe now I'm ready to put an ad in the personals, you know . . . something like: forty-one-year-old nurse, tall, good-looking and jovial, looking for man of same age to share pleasant moments with, etc."

"You'll get all the weirdos wanting to wear a nurse's uniform," John says and smiles at the thought.

She giggles. "Or, forty-one-year-old nurse from PEI, with rather large

159

mercury thermometer, looking to take temperature. Men with hairy backsides need not respond."

They laugh together.

She takes off her glasses and places them on the newspaper, rubbing her eyes.

"How's your Thoughts-of-the-Day going, eh?" She nudges him on the arm playfully.

"I started this thing today . . . It's about a brown suitcase . . . I have a brown suitcase too, actually. A hand-me-down, really old. I came to Canada with it."

"Tell me then . . . "

"I don't want to tell you before it's finished, but you can tell me what you think when it's done . . . "

"Why a suitcase?"

"I don't know . . . I was thinking about life and people and how ephemeral everything is about us . . . An object, like a suitcase, for instance, may be around for a hundred years, right? But the people who used it probably won't. So, you may look at an object as a thing that serves a generic purpose, yet it can also be the mute depository of life events, emotions, dreams, moments . . . "

She says, "Like, if a suitcase could talk, sort of thing?"

"Hmm . . ." He continues, "the world is filled with billions of objects, right? There are probably more objects than human beings and animals combined on earth, at any given time, if you think about it . . . Anyway, it's something like this . . . the idea . . . Imagine a Museum of Random Objects, where you would see Dr Weinberg's beloved bed, and the reading glasses of Anne from Prince Edward Island, the photo of Mary's cousin, John's toaster, someone's fireplace, a piece of wall, you know, totally random objects . . . a recording would tell you stories about all these things. It could also be called the Museum of Really Boring Things, depending . . . "

"You are the most unusual person I know, John. I mean, this idea, who would ever think of it? It would never occur to me." She shakes her head in astonishment.

"It's probably a totally absurd thought, kind of stupid, that's why, but anyway . . . "

He is uncomfortable now and wants to change the subject.

"So what's new on the floor?" he asks.

"Your Dragon Lady is on crutches now, spent hours walking up and down the corridor, trying to get used to them. 'Daughtah from Vancouvah' is here, waiting for her to get better so she can take her there. Her grandson is a cute boy, very polite."

"Ben?"

"Still fighting for his life in Intensive Care. His father came a second time, stood watching at the foot of his bed. Ben slept through the whole thing."

"I should go check on the Dragon Lady." John gets up and walks quietly down the corridor. When he peeks in, he finds Mrs Liu looking at pictures. She looks up: "Come!"

He goes to the side of her bed. "Xiao, here. Grandson." She gives him a photograph of the boy.

"He looks happy."

"Yes, apple-face grandson. Very good boy. A little stupid, but good."

"Why do you say that?" he asks.

"Wants make moving drawing. Moving drawing . . . " She makes a grimace.

"He's a budding artist, you should be proud!"

"I make fish. Help brain . . . " she taps her forehead with her index finger.

John chuckles. "So, when are you leaving Montreal?"

"Two days . . . Thank you."

"For what? Didn't do anything . . . "

She nods. "Thank you. Goodbye."

"Good luck," he says and leaves the room, waving back at her.

He takes the elevator to the ICU where he looks in at Ben from behind a glass pane. There is a man also watching, in a dark suit, holding a briefcase. He stands further away from the window, immobile, impassive. Tubes snake in and out of the young man's body. One large accordion tube covers the boy's face, helping him breathe through a mask. His soft elongated fingers lie curled up by his side. The man in the dark suit brings his hands together in front of him, still holding the briefcase, and gazes through the window.

"They will let you in, if you ask," John says to him. "You're his father, aren't you?"

The man turns briefly to look at him, but says nothing. A little later he departs, his footsteps echoing down the tiled corridor. John heads for the elevator.

℮

When he looks up from his notebook, it is already past midnight. Most of the lights on the floor have been turned off, leaving him in the glowing heat of the desk lamp. He rises, stretching his legs, and looks around for Anne, who has disappeared for her midnight nap. He sits back down, putting his feet on the desk, holding the back of his head with his crossed hands. There is a coughing to the left of the hallway, an old tired cough. He puts his feet down, waiting for it to subside, ready to spring up and hurry down the hall to find out. Silence returns. John catches a glimpse of his face reflected from the pen holder on the desk. It is a broken reflection, he moves his head to find his eyes feeling a profound unease at not seeing his own eyes in this vague image of himself. He tries to imagine a life without eyes, without any sort of visual reference to one's presence. The nose one breathes through, versus the longish extension dividing the face in half with its small twists and bumps, the nostrils, the curve of the lips, the colour of the forehead, a blemish, a birthmark. All this subtracted from the self. He finds the two deep grooves dividing his forehead in half. He plays with his reflection for a while longer, moving the holder this way and that, delighting in distortions. The cough returns, this time louder. He puts the holder down, waiting. It is a man's cough, and reminds him of Romeo Fournier. It oc-

curs to him that he is perhaps the only person left in the world who remembers Romeo's existence. He gets up and goes to the elevator, takes
it down to the Fridge. Amato is reading the newspaper on the desk, while
listening to late night jazz on the radio.

"Hey Amato, how are you doing, man?"

"Okay, okay . . . What's up, man?"

"Nothing much . . . I was thinking of the old guy, Romeo Fournier,
remember, the man in the Fridge . . . What happened to him? Did anyone
claim . . . ?"

"Man, there are hundreds of stiffs in these drawers, and you expect
me to remember names? What do you care, anyway?"

"I don't know . . . I felt sorry for the guy, dying up there all alone. Did
anyone come for his body?"

Amato gets up slowly, opens a large drawer in the file cabinet, and
takes out the registry.

"Let's see . . . " He places the thick oversized book on top of his newspaper. "Only for you, man. Only 'cause you're a nice guy. Don't tell anyone I showed you it. Don't get me into trouble . . . "

"I know, I know. Won't tell anyone. Can't stop thinking about this old
man for some reason. I'll feel better if I know someone came for him."

"What was his name again?"

"Romeo Fournier."

Amato slides his finger down the page and turns it. He is about to
turn the second page when he stops at the bottom.

"Here he is. Fournier, Romeo. Let me see . . . Some residence requested a death certificate, it looks like. Hold on . . . "

He goes back to the filing cabinet and takes out another large book.
He puts it on the desk and slides his finger down another list.

"Yeah. Organ donation. There is a list here. Crematorium. Same residence requested we send it there; here, see it?" He points at the name.

"I see," says John. "If no one claims the ashes what happens to
them?"

"What do I know, man? I work at the hospital morgue, not some funeral parlour!"

"Yeah, sorry. I thought you might know . . . "

Amato closes the books and returns them to the cabinet.

"I would think they'd keep them in a box, in a drawer or something. Did this guy not have anyone?"

"Dunno . . . No one came to visit him . . . "

"If he was poor, I don't think the residence would pay for extra costs like keeping his ashes and so on. I'm just guessing . . . "

"A bit depressing, eh?"

"You bet . . . You just ruined the comics section." Amato points at the newspaper. "Now I'll have to do the crossword puzzle. I hate that shit."

"Then don't do it."

"What else is there to do? I read everything already. Even the obituaries . . . "

"Bring a book or something."

"Yeah, something like that . . . Maybe play games on the computer. No one ever comes here, anyway, except you. Freak!" Amato laughs, revealing a gold tooth.

"Fuck you!" John smiles. "I'll bring my backgammon set tomorrow."

"So I can play by myself?"

"No, we play during my breaks . . . If you're not sleeping."

As he enters the elevator, an idea occurs to him. Jeanette Daoust. He will place a small ad in the personals, advising her of Romeo Fournier's death. He rushes to his desk, composes a small ad in French and calls the newspaper. The ad will appear the next day, the clerk tells him. It will cost $17.86.

~

Across the Atlantic Ocean at the far end of Europe, a radio clock goes off at seven o'clock in the morning. There is a jingle, voices, a traffic report in Greek delivered by a man with a deep voice. Thomas opens his eyes, feeling disoriented, still half asleep. He lies on his back immobile, wanting to piece together the dream that's quickly vanishing in the morning light, as the radio cuts into his thoughts with a jumble of voices, music, and artificial cheerfulness. He will soon rise and prepare breakfast, wake up the children, drive them to school and go to his office; but not yet. He turns to his side, staring at the clock digits adding up. He decides to wait until an attractive number comes up, a number divisible many times; twenty, perhaps. Twenty-one, the sleeker but more capricious number, would give him one more minute in bed. He hesitates, finally settling on twenty. His ex-wife is definitely a twenty-one. He stares at the red digits on the clock. Still at seventeen, so three more minutes. And September? Possibly a twenty. If twenty were a colour would it be yellow? He closes his eyes. When he opens them again it is 7:22. He gets up and shuffles to the bathroom.

Breakfast is a quiet affair, the two teenagers chewing bread with eyes half closed, sleep having puffed their faces. Thomas sips his coffee as he walks back and forth in the apartment, retrieving files and looking for a tie, his greying hair combed back and sleek. Soon they leave, the youngsters in their navy blue uniforms crumpled under their packsacks. Their father appears more energetic to them since their return home, his gait bouncier as he walks around the front of the car and reaches for his door. Margaret stares at the back of his neck once he sits down, her sense of outrage curving her lips down. *He seems happier with my mother gone.* She glances sideways at Robert, who is looking out the window with unfocused eyes, observing something invisible to all but him. *Robert never notices anything.* She sighs, feeling angry and abandoned by him. Thomas turns on the radio. He flips channels to find something to suit his mood. Bits of voices, music, and static burst into the air.

"Stop it, dad! Stop it! This is so annoying!"

He glances quickly through the mirror. "You want me to turn it off?"

"Yes. I hate it when you do that."

He shuts it off, exiting the oleander-lined fragrant road down into a sunny chaos of honks, noise, and exhaust in the midst of a traffic jam.

"This is going nowhere . . . ," Thomas sighs, staring out the window.

He feels the heat of the sun on his left arm, light bouncing off all surfaces, the side mirrors, his glasses, the cars in front. His mind drifts towards Montreal, and September, with her particular shade of yellow in a city that bears its thirst for sunlight with stoic elegance, waiting for the ever elusive proof of spring to arrive in slim, slanted rays upon its frigid sidewalks. September in her transparent lemonade uniform, and white mask, her mass of chestnut hair bouncing in a ponytail. Like a flight attendant in a space cartoon, she walks up and down for him in a narrow aisle between jammed cars, swinging her hips ever so slightly with each step. Once in a while she turns around and looks at him with that direct, almost harsh gaze. She turns back, walking carefully between the cars, eyes upon a faraway spot in the horizon, somewhere beyond the vehicles and fumes, where a young couple is playing with a water hose in a garden. She stops to watch and he can see her yearning for joy fix into that distant, invisible place where the couple continues to play, where it is always summer, where the moment of laughter is eternal . . .

Cars start inching along, shifting the spaces between them. His vision of September disappears.

"Where were you just now?" asks his daughter from the back.

"Who? Me?" Startled, he looks at her in his mirror.

"Yes, you, dad. You were not in the car with us."

He smiles. "Heaven, maybe."

"Huh?"

"Nothing . . . Just had a thought. Here we go. Cars are starting to move." He shifts gears.

"What's heaven like, then?" She moves forward with interest.

"Well, for one thing, it's not like this!" He moves the shift stick impatiently and accelerates, entering the steady flow of traffic.

"You give non-answers. Mom doesn't do that."

"That's because mom's a lot smarter."

"No. You can't be bothered to share anything."

"Okay, stop right here. I could share that you're a pain in the neck right now." He gives her a toothy smile through the mirror. She looks away, frowning, lips in a compressed line.

"Don't be mad at me all the time! Okay, what's heaven like, let's see . . . I had this thought just now, that heaven is the infinite repetition of a moment containing a thought or an illusion of beauty, or happiness your mind plays out in order to," his hand leaves the steering wheel for a flourish in the air, "torture and seduce you. It wouldn't be torture if it didn't seduce you, and it wouldn't be seductive if there was no cause for torture. It entices you along, like a poor fish going for the worm on a hook."

He stops, revisiting the thought.

"What's hell like then?" Robert's uneven voice resonates in the car suddenly.

"Good God, that's one heavy start for a regular school day!"

Thomas looks at Robert sitting beside him, sober, unaware of the tiny smudge of red jam dried up on the side of his mouth.

"I think I'll have to think of that one a little harder, Robert . . . It's too complicated for my poor brain."

"I suppose," offers Robert, "it's a loop which brings torture without seduction. The fish already knows it's destined for the frying pan."

Thomas manoeuvres the car to the side of the road and stops. He caresses his son's head. "Sounds depressing enough . . . Here," he offers his handkerchief, "there's a bit of jam there."

Robert quickly wipes the side of his mouth with it and opens the door to leave.

Thomas waits for the teenagers to disappear into the concrete school building. Margaret turns and waves at him, her face still serious. As he starts his car, September enters his mind once more, walking into his view with her small featureless boy whom he has never met. She sits next to him in the car, still wearing the uniform and mask. She lifts her left arm and stretches it over the back of her seat, so that the shadow of her armpit is visible through the short sleeve. The thought of that small sliver of warm skin overwhelms him with lust. An impatient honk awakens him as he slowly merges into the highway, a car among thousands flowing in unison. He returns to her arm slung over the back of her seat lifting an invisible breast concealed under layers of clothing. Her eyes are vague still, looking through him, through the smog and the river of cars to some distant point, immobile and silent, a breathing stillness of herself. He knows this image of her will haunt him wherever he goes. She will enter his mind in the midst of a meeting, while shaving, or crossing streets. She will lift her head just so, her lips will pout, her arm will draw a careless arc and he will be transfixed with desire. Life will lose its usual references. The visible world will beckon the ghost of her; a silhouette here, a gaze there, until it is completely conquered by her illusion.

℮

When the phone rings in the small street-level apartment on Henri-Julien Street, September is in the bathroom, her mouth filled with foam and toothbrush. She is bent over the sink carefully, so as not to stain her clothes with dribbles of toothpaste, her wavy brown hair spread on her back like a rolling hillside. It is six-thirty in the morning. She quickly rinses her mouth when she hears the second ring, and in her rush to get the phone she stains her dress.

"Yes?" she shouts into the receiver out of breath.

"Thomas here . . . "

"Oh! I didn't expect . . . Where are you calling from?"

"Athens . . . I'm really missing your uniform with the little mask on top of your head."

He hears a chuckle.

"Do you want me to order one for you?"

"Do they come in my size?" He smiles as her laughter spreads into his ear, then down his chest. "I had this idea to invite you to Athens with your little boy . . . You know, spend a week or two here, a vacation. I could arrange for your plane, your hotel and everything, you just need to show up . . . How does this sound? A little crazy, but doable . . . No?"

September sits heavily on her bed, looking at the stain on her dress. "It's really generous of you and everything . . . I'm not sure why you're doing it. I mean, I don't even . . . "

He interrupts, "Know you . . . I know, you do like to remind me of this often. How will you ever know me if you're there and I'm here? It's no big deal, you know . . . A holiday with your kid. It just happens to be in Greece and you happen to know me here."

"And I happen to owe you the entire trip . . . I can't . . . "

"If it doesn't work, you go back and forget about it. I won't bother you at all. I promise. I'm an honourable man."

He waits, eyes fixed on the white ceiling of his office. A spider jumps from the light fixture and hangs in space tied to its own thread. He is surprised by the "honourable man" part of his own speech, momentarily worried she'll discount him as an old-fashioned fool.

Her eyes wander around the room. "I need to get ready for work now. I'll call you later."

She gets up, throws a look at Eric, who remembers to lift his filled spoon to his mouth.

e⌒

John gets off Bus 144, slowly walks down the street towards his apartment, his eyes burning with fatigue. September opens her yellow door and steps into the greenish early morning light that bounces off young fresh leaves growing on treetops like new hair. He sees her silhouette against the sun, the skirt moulding her hips, the chestnut hair bouncing with every high-heeled step.

"September!" he calls. "September, wait!" He runs towards her, waving his hand. She turns around, a hand shielding her squinting eyes from the sun. He reaches her side, slightly out of breath, fumbling inside his packsack.

"Salvador . . . left an envelope for you. Has he called you at all?"

"No." He cannot tell from her face if she wanted him to or not. "You?"

"Just left me a letter. I don't have his address or phone number."

She nods. "I don't think he'll call me . . . If he does, I'll let you know."

She waves and walks away toward Carré St-Louis, where the hard brown crusts of trees once covered in snow have burgeoned all at once. A city truck is parked beside the fountain. A gardener in orange overalls carefully unloads his plants from the truck in preparation for planting. John, watching the square covered in the damp morning haze, sees the silhouette of woman and child walking towards the bronze water fountain, remembers the snowy day when September was still a complete stranger he was hoping to court. It occurs to him in those few seconds standing there that life, with all its mornings, evenings, and mysteries is a fluid; a silent current made of water and blood flowing unseen through everything, incessantly, a current we tirelessly attempt to hinder with houses and roads and objects, like so many pebbles in a stream, until it is all carried and washed away. September and Eric disappear as they cross the park towards the subway.

e⌐

"This computer, once I'm done with it, will be good as new. You'll chat with your children in Athens, and perhaps even find old friends that have long disappeared into the world . . . you know. It'll be good, I promise." Inga Lundsgard is on her knees screwing back together the case of a computer. Her cheeks are flushed as she looks up at Selma, who has walked into the living room with coffee cups.

"You really like fixing stuff, don't you?" she says.

"I like to see things work," replies Inga from the floor. "Not true: I like to see things not work, so I can make them work . . . It relaxes me. So, I go around fixing computers, toasters, radios, anything . . . I can stick together a broken vase, too. If you ever have one . . . "

"You're lucky you're good at something. I'm not particularly good at anything."

"Maybe you haven't given yourself a chance to find out . . . " Inga rises, turning on the computer to see if it works.

"I want to do some gardening. Maybe then I'll find the courage to plant things, become a farmer. There is so much land here. I have time now . . . " She takes a sip of her coffee. "I have been wearing jeans and sweat pants since I came here. The closet is full of fancy dresses and skirts . . . Whatever for?" She inquires with a smile.

"For going to the city more often; you're turning into a recluse here in the countryside."

"I don't mind it terribly . . . I feel like a stranger. It's just hitting me now, I guess."

Inga sits on the sofa, momentarily forgetting the computer.

"Listen, Selma, this, your grandma's house, is a refuge. Where's your life?"

She kneels back down, unscrewing the box once again, stealing a glance towards the other end of the living room, where Arvid is sitting on the carpet by the fireplace, humming a tune as he plays with the wooden blocks they found in the attic. They date from Fru Selma's childhood. He manipulates the pieces with care, because they belong to ancient times and very old people, like parents and Vivaldi.

"I see myself growing old here, just like my grandma, my children and grandchildren spending summer vacations with me, taking walks in the forest, this place being their refuge from all the demands of life. Perhaps, this is my life, you know, to be the guardian of this place until I pass it on."

"You speak of this farmhouse as something that will continue to be in your lineage for generations. Most likely, your children will sell it when you're gone, as you almost did when your grandmother passed away."

"You may be right . . . But to me, now, this is the place where my grandmother's spirit resides. Every step I take, everywhere I look I'm reminded of this."

"So you live in a shrine?"

"Is that wrong?"

"No . . . , " Inge says pensively, then pushes a button and waits for a sound, which fails to come. "Maybe, a bit lonely . . . Is that what you want?" She shakes her head. "This part is definitely not working. I'll need to get another one."

"I don't know. My life . . . I recently realized this: from a young age I somehow avoided doing what I truly wanted, thinking I truly wanted what I was doing. And what I did . . . there was no plan, you know. There was no understanding of where I'd be, say, today . . . Or of how I felt versus how I wanted to feel. It's all such a muddle . . . Actually, I never had an anchor except this house, my grandma. My parents were both egocentric. I mean, I couldn't count on them to stop for me. Then they died in that crash, and from never being able to count on them, I was suddenly crushed by the burden of their disappearance. I resented them for dying like that, and leaving me to sort out their messes. All I wanted to do before they died was follow this guy to Canada. Some stupid dream probably. He was from the wrong side of town. He had a history, you know. I couldn't imagine telling my parents about him, let alone follow him anywhere. He took off, and they crashed. Overnight, I . . . Well . . . Thomas was good to me, in the end. We had the appearance of a good thing, and it was fine too, in a way. It's weird, you know, when you lose your parents and you're young, it's as if suddenly you want to live their lives for them and change the script so they can do it right, for you. Meanwhile, it's your life and you're just messing it up. How I talk! Sorry, Inga. I'm boring you."

"No, you're not. Keep going . . . "

"I guess we carry different messes forward, trying to fix old ones. So, your kids will focus on avoiding your mistakes while making others, and so on. And I think, yes, I succeeded where my mother failed. But I failed to give them a notion of happiness, because I didn't even bother to look for it . . . I'm so tired, Inga . . . "

"Maybe happiness is overrated."

"You're saying this because you're happy."

"Not really."

"Then why?"

"Because doing the right thing is more important, and it may not be a happy thing."

"How do you know you've done the right thing?"

"I have no idea . . . Why did he move to Canada, this guy?"

"Not sure. Some of his friends from university ended up in jail. One committed suicide. He never got over that. He felt he'd be next, I suppose. He wanted a new life."

"I think I have the right piece for this thing at home." Inga says and gets up, rearranging her small tool kit. "Arvid?"

 ℯ

John feels salty water touch his lips. When he opens his eyes, he realizes he is afloat in the sea, the sun beating down on his shoulders and hurting his eyes as it reflects back to his face from the blue mass. He squints. From a distance echoes of children playing and shrieking arrive, mixed with the motor sounds of a fishing boat. A seagull passes. He moves his arms and legs in the clear water, thinking, *I'm home, I'm home, at last.* There is no land in sight. It doesn't matter. He joyfully flaps his arms and legs in the translucent turquoise sea, splashing water in his own face. He thinks, *I will lie on my back and float until I reach the shore. I will let the water carry me.* He opens his arms and legs as if doing a cartwheel on his back. The sun burns his salty lips. His body floats partly submerged in cool water. He smiles, letting the sea rock his limbs. The soft voice of a woman hums in his ears, some song, a lullaby that he recognizes. It slowly invades everything; the puffy clouds carved out of the bright sky, the seagull that crosses above his head, the vast sea, the foam on the water, even the skin beneath his fingernails. He closes his eyes and awakens in his apartment on Henri-Julien. School children are walking down the street, their young voices getting fainter as they walk away. The telephone rings. He lets it ring three, four times before picking it up. An old woman's voice enters his ear. *It's about the ad in the paper,* she says. *I am Jeannette Daoust.* He sits back on his crumpled bed cover. *I'm sorry to hear about Romeo. He used to be a good friend. I wish I had known.* He asks her where she is calling from. *I live in Montreal, she says. With my daughter.* Mr Fournier was asking for you the day he died, he says. Silence at the other end. There is a sigh, more silence. He had a picture of you. I think he would have wanted you to have it back. *Would you like me to mail it to you? Are you a relative?* I work at the hospital where he died. I took care of him, the last few days . . . *I can meet you for a coffee,* she offers reluctantly. *My daughter will be with me.* She tells him where.

John takes down the address; somewhere on Gouin Avenue, north of the city. Probably close to where she lives, he concludes as he hangs up the receiver and lies back down, his heart thudding in his ears and chest.

℮

The diner is one of the old ones that has not yet transformed into a coffee franchise. The patrons are mostly retirees, grimly sipping coffee from thick white mugs. The seats are brown vinyl, long padded benches along the walls, facing Formica tables. He looks around for two women who may look like mother and daughter, a burgundy coat, white hair. He sits down, concluding they have not yet arrived, and orders tea. There is no music in the background, and he can hear assorted bits of conversation rising from nearby tables, and the jarring noise of dishes and cutlery.

Jeannette Daoust is meanwhile sitting by a window at the other end of the diner waiting for a sign. Her burgundy coat is carefully folded beside her seat. She is wearing pearl earrings. Her white hair is styled into a wavy bob around her neck. A pearl necklace encircles the collar of a lilac dress. She looks around the restaurant for a face that may be John's, sees a thin man with very dark smooth hair that flaps over his forehead as he looks down at his cup, stirring its contents. At first he looks boyish to her. Then she realizes he could be in his late thirties or early forties. He is wearing jeans, a navy blue sweater, a leather jacket. She keeps looking at him, waiting for him to see her once he lifts his head.

When he does, his eyes meet her insistent gaze. He rises and walks towards her table.

"Madame Daoust?"

She nods.

"Je suis Jean," he stretches out his hand which she takes and squeezes

174

very slightly.

"Assieds-toi, Jean. We can speak English, it's okay."

"Your daughter?"

"She'll be here soon. I was a little nervous about meeting a stranger like this . . . I have wondered about Romeo over the years. The way I saw your ad was funny. First of all, I never read the personals. Don't know why I did this time, I was having my coffee and just started reading. Your ad was second or third from the top. I think if it had been towards the middle of the page we would have never met . . . Do you want to tell me about Romeo?"

"I don't have a lot to tell. He was very ill. He was very angry about it. He asked us to call his wife, at the end. We couldn't find her on the admission form. I somehow figured he didn't have a wife in the legal sense. After his death, I went to the hospice where he had lived before the hospital and visited his room. He had a framed picture of you. Here it is."

He pulls out the picture from the inside pocket of his jacket and hands it to her.

"I will go get my tea. I left it at my table over there." He gets up and leaves the table momentarily, returning with his cup.

"It is quite awkward, isn't it?" The old woman says looking up from the picture. "Here we are, complete strangers, and you hand me this memento of myself from a man you hardly knew. You must meet so many people in distress, doing your job, and yet, here you are. If you were his son, I would think you were looking for answers about his life. Are you looking for something or just being kind? Est-ce le bon mot, 'kind'?"

"I don't know . . . I just felt the picture needed to find its home, to be in the right hands. It felt so sad, to visit that room, see his few belongings and that picture of you in the midst of all that. He lived for it, it seemed. It means something to you . . . " He waits, then continues, "I don't think he had children. I think he wanted to find you. He wanted you to be his wife. I don't know what good this does . . . " He looks at his bony hands crossed in front of him on the table. They feel cold. "No one came to visit him. No one claimed his remains. He was old and fragile and filled with suffering. I had to try to find you. I'm sorry if I've disturbed you by doing this . . . "

"No, no, Jean . . . You did the right thing. I will need to spend some time alone with this picture. Before my daughter returns. Actually she's sitting over there. She didn't want to get in the way." Her somewhat deformed index finger points subtly in the direction of an overweight blond woman with glasses wearing faded jeans and a pink sweatshirt, bent over a newspaper a few tables away. Jeannette's skin is paper-thin on her fingers, he notes, as he moves his eyes towards the daughter.

"She doesn't look much like you," he says now, thinking of the young woman in the picture.

"No, she takes after her father. She has my colours, though . . . Would you like to meet her?"

"Let's not disturb her. I should get going. You want to spend some time alone." He stands up.

"Yes," she says, her hand reaching for his. She holds on to it a little as he moves away. "Thank you for doing this."

She watches the slight, dark-haired man leave the restaurant and disappear behind the door. The faded memory of a man from long ago, the young cobbler who worked across from the coffee shop on Mansfield Street, returns. She goes over that encounter in the blizzard, the contents of her purse scattered in the fresh snow. The lipstick implanted into a white mound next to the small powder box half sunk in the softness. The keys already invisible having fallen through the snow. The young man rushing out of his shop in slippers, his socks getting wet, lifting her up, then gathering the scattered objects one by one and handing them to her. From his gaze, she knew he was already in love with her. She had a moment's regret as he smiled through the swirling flakes, holding her. There it was, the possibility of something breathless unfolding if she allowed that smile a return, that instant. Instead, she looked down and mumbled a shy thank you. Could one instant in a snowstorm define one's entire life? She looks at the blue veins running through her fingers, the two gold wedding rings, now loose, the manicured nails around the picture, like claws. Before, she could imagine Romeo somewhere in the world remembering their blizzard. She is alone now, holding this torn photograph, relic of the love that never was. Jeannette places the torn picture carefully in her purse and rises from her seat, waving at her daughter to come and join her.

*

John goes straight to work from the restaurant. He visits Intensive Care, to see Ben, who's hooked up to an IV drip, oxygen tubes, and a heart monitor. The young man's eyes are open, he looks up at John as he comes near him wearing a mask.

"Nurse Ratchett," he whispers.

"How are you feeling, kid?"

"Lucky," Ben tries a half smile.

"Got any visitors?"

"My old man . . . everyday."

"Talk to him?"

"I pretend . . . " he sighs, " . . . to sleep."

"Don't want him there?"

Ben closes his eyes, says nothing.

"You'd better sleep, kid." John pats his shoulder gently. "I'll come again later."

"Sure, nurse . . . "

*

Later Anne tells him Ben should move out of Intensive Care and to their floor in a couple of days until he is stable enough to be taken to psychiatric care. Mrs Liu was taken home by her daughter earlier, she adds, giving him an account of other events on the floor.

"She left this for you, by the way." She hands him a paper bag containing something. "She didn't have anything to put it in, so I gave her the bag. Here . . . "

He finds a box with two navy blue metal balls inside, one decorated with a golden dragon and the other with a phoenix, and they seem to be the same ones that he had seen inside her red dragon bag.

"Aren't they supposed to be good for pain or something?" Anne asks.

"Baoding balls," he says, "for vital energy to move through the body."

He removes them from the box and rolls them around in his palms, enjoying their smooth round mass.

"I'm feeling great already," he winks at her. "Try it."

"Whatever happened to your suitcase story?" she asks, rolling the balls in her palm.

"I think it ended on me."

"You mean you finished it."

"No, I mean it kind of ran out."

"I don't know what that means."

"Oh well, we'll see what happens. If a story is about a suitcase, at some point it runs out of movement, you know, unless someone puts a ticking bomb in it that explodes. No more suitcase, no more story . . . That's one way of getting rid of it neatly. Well, not so neatly, depending on the damage it causes. Maybe that's what I should do. Transfer the suitcase away from people searching for their lives to someone who's already decided to waste his for some greater cause, you know, country, religion, ideology, war, something along those lines. From the moment he takes hold of my old brown leather suitcase, this poor sod knows its future destination: garbage. But what matters to him is not the future of the suitcase, obviously. Day and night he thinks about the bomb. He has these moments of profound doubt and terror when he's tempted to pack his shorts and go on a vacation instead. But no, he belongs to a group and they keep reminding him of the war, the cause, the injustice, fuelling his anger and despair. He has nightmares about scooping up pieces of his own brain and organs from the sidewalk. The night before he does the deed, he has the same nightmare again, except this time instead of shreds of his own flesh, he finds his heart, intact, right there on the sidewalk, pumping among the debris. He hears the thudding in his ears, and feels it in his chest, even though it's sitting there on concrete, bleeding away. He picks it up and starts running down the street howling for someone to call an ambulance, so his heart can be saved."

Anne has stopped rolling the balls in her chubby palms, her mouth hangs open.

"That's it?"

"Yep. Done. Are you hungry? I feel like having sushi . . . "

"How can that be it? Can he do the deed after such a dream?"

"That's not a suitcase story. You take it from there. I'm done with mine."

"Where's your mortadella sandwich?"

"Not here."

"You can run to Le Faubourg and get us sushi. I'll cover here. Take a taxi, faster . . . Let me give you some money."

John shakes his head and rushes to the elevator, leaving Anne in a pensive mood, rolling Mrs Liu's baoding balls in her hand.

When John returns with a platter of sushi and chopsticks, he finds Anne sitting alone in the bright spherical light of the table lamp by the desk. The illumination makes a shadow on part of her face, accentuating the lines from the sides of her nose to her lips. There is the faint sound of radio music and beeping from distant monitors.

"John, it bothers me. Tell me what happens to the guy the next day."

John's laughter ends in a snort.

"Geez, Anne . . . I don't know. He packs his shorts and moves to another continent where he hopes to live in peace. That okay? Let's eat."

"Are you the bomb guy?"

He stops the piece of sushi a few inches away from his mouth.

"No. I'm not."

He shoves the sushi in his mouth and chews, suddenly annoyed.

"Don't get sore . . . So who is the bomb guy?"

"How do I know?"

"You've imagined him, obviously."

"What difference does it make? If you want a story about the bomb guy, you're welcome to write it yourself."

"Do you like the ginger thing?" she points at the slices of ginger pickle.

"No, you have it."

Her chopsticks advance into the take-out container like the beak of a crane and squeeze the small pink mound, lifting it up in the air.

"Why do you get irritated with me when I ask you stuff?"

As she says this, she sees a sudden softening in John's eyes, something like realization. He smiles.

"I don't get irritated with *you,* I just get irritated . . . I don't know why. Listen, Anne, all these years we've worked together, we're friends. What you tell me, I accept. But with me, you're filled with question marks, as if what I tell you is not good enough and I just find it a bit tiresome. That's all. For instance, I don't think I've ever asked you why you left the Maritimes to come here. Right? Whatever your reasons were, if it was a good thing for you, it's okay by me. I'm not an enigma you need to solve, you know. I'm just this guy, John, I care for people and hook up their IVs just like you do, I like to write in my notebook, you like to knit . . . whatever. Do you know what I mean? I tell you a story, you wonder if it's about me. Why should it be? Why should I be a bomb guy?"

"You just don't talk about yourself at all. I do. I tell you about this guy I loved, right? I tell you about my brother and my childhood, okay? You don't ask me, I tell you. Why not? But you, it's as if there's no continuity. What did you do before this? Who were you before this? I know nothing about you. So I wonder, did he run away from something? I can't help it."

"I'm just not a very talkative guy who lives what basically amounts to a very ordinary life. I have coffee in the mornings, I pay my bills, I come to work, I don't like cleaning my fridge, I have a few friends. The only difference is maybe that while I go through the motions of this uneventful life, in my head there's another more eventful one. I can't tell you why, I don't know . . . What do you want to know about my childhood? I'll tell you this: I grew up an only child. I don't know my father. He took off. My mother was a crushed, bitter woman. I basically ruined her life by coming into the world . . . Her family pushed her away, and so I have no extended family. Anyway, the whole thing was quite sad, I guess, except when we went to the movies. It's the one thing we did together that felt good. Side by side in a dark theatre, absorbed in imaginary lives, not our own. She died, I went to university and here I am. Point is, did you really need to know all this, to understand me better? I don't think so. Do you think I don't fit in because I was born elsewhere, or do you expect that I shouldn't fit in despite the fact that I do? I'll tell you who doesn't fit in. That kid in intensive care who's been drugging himself to death since he was twelve. That kid doesn't fit in. And why is that?"

"I never thought you didn't 'fit in', whatever that means. C'mon man, you speak perfect French, I can't even do that! I just don't feel I know enough about you, after a decade or so and it strikes me as a strange thing. It's not at all about belonging or not. That whole theme is an obsession of yours, isn't it?"

"Anne, I don't really have a lot to tell. The other day, I had this memory, it was so vivid, of the gritty texture of the concrete wall surrounding the school yard. It came up to my chest, and I remember pressing my hands on its edge, looking at the world outside. I must have spent quite a bit of time doing that during recess. My fingertips and palms would turn red, with tiny bumps and grooves imprinted in them. I'd look at passersby, wondering which one looked like me, which one was my father. You're a kid, you figure out your dad was not worth knowing because of what you hear all the time, yet somewhere in your mind you keep an alternate father who is unsoiled by his deeds, the one who'd be walking down the street and looking down, noticing your face above the concrete wall of the school yard and coming to your rescue, having a morally adequate explanation for his absence, of course. You know, the one who is not a jerk and kisses your cheeks when you weep. I spent a lot of time with that father, in my mind. I mean, who wants to spend time with an imaginary jerk, right? Then one day they both disappeared; the jerk and the kind stranger. One day I must have realized, well, I'm fatherless, and this is how the fatherless live."

His chopsticks grasp a piece of sushi.

"So are you going to eat?" he nudges her with his elbow.

She nods, picks up a piece of salmon sushi. She slips it into her mouth and chews it pensively. They sit in the light of the desk lamp chewing while distant voices trickle out from under closed doors, elevators ring their floors, a subdued cough or a moan bursts into the deepening night.

e

What they do not yet know is that Ben will be wheeled past their desk and into room 417 sometime between 10:30 and 11:00 AM the next day, while they are off their shifts, sleeping at home. He will be told that he is expected to recuperate under observation for a few days before being moved to another hospital, for psychiatric care. Ben will sit on his bed squinting in the bright morning light, looking down at the city below, wondering what to do with his limbs now that they are able to move, apprehensive about his father's visit yet again before the end of the day. *Either you kill yourself or you keep moving. Either you kill yourself or you keep moving. Either you kill yourself . . .* He stops his mind mid loop. I keep moving. I feel the misery. I keep moving. Moving where? *Either you . . .* A nurse will walk in, doe-eyed and young and sparkling with dreams in her fresh uniform. She will notice his hands shaking.

"Are you all right?" she will ask.

"No . . . ," he will say. "My mind is racing. I need it to stop. Sedate me. Find me something. I feel really bad. I want to die." He will start pacing up and down, next to his bed, tears running down his cheeks. *Either you . . .*

"Please sit down, I will go find a doctor." She will feel nervous as she rushes out to get someone, this situation not found in her textbook.

A psychiatrist will come, thin, tall, with wrinkled skin hanging over the hard-edged shirt collar as if they had stretched him up and down and forgotten about his neck. Above the creases, a shiny bald head will tower in the shape of an egg. *Either you kill yourself or you keep moving.* "I don't know how to keep moving," Ben will blurt out to the psychiatrist, who will nod his large egg without saying anything.

Does he understand or does he pretend to, does he care or does he pretend to? "I don't know what to do in this room. I think I should get out."

"I cannot let you out right now. I'll give you something to calm you down." He will write on his pad. The nurse will wheel in the IV pole, she will awkwardly search for a vein, tapping here and there, sweat gathering around her hairline, until she finds it and sticks the needle in apologetically. She will adjust the pole, hang the transparent pouch and the various tubes through which medicine will flow into his blood stream, blurring his thoughts. She will fidget around him for a while, making sure he is calmer and leave the room.

Ben will lie in bed once more, eyes closed. When the tired-looking middle-aged nurse on the following shift walks into his room hours later, he will say to her, "I don't want to be awake. Give me something to sleep. I don't want my father to visit; tell him to leave if he shows up." He will then turn his head towards the window to watch the green belt of forest between the mountain and the skyscrapers and grey smog down below, untouched by the fresh, bright colours of spring. *You keep moving. You keep moving. But how? Where?*

He will fall asleep and dream of running with his eyes bandaged. Out of breath, he will try to tear off the bandage as he keeps running. There is danger approaching but he doesn't know what, he just has to keep going faster and faster. Without a bandage over his eyes, he realizes he still cannot see. He will awaken with a gasp, feeling a light touch on his arm, and find the male nurse from the cemetery by the side of his bed.

"Were you chasing me?" he will mumble, disoriented.

"I woke you up."

"I dreamt I was running, blind. Someone was chasing me."

"You're soaked . . . Must have been some chase. Do you want me to help you change your gown?"

"Yeah, later. When did you come?"

"An hour ago. I hear you slept the entire day."

"Did . . . he come to visit?"

"He did. You were sleeping so I didn't bother telling him to leave."

"Was he just standing there again with his stupid briefcase?"

"Without it, this time."

"Will you give me something to sleep?"

"Nothing was prescribed."

"Go find Dr Egghead. Tell him I want to sleep."

"You sure his name is Dr Egghead?"

"Whatever. Find me a doctor. Get me a prescription."

"Why do you want to sleep so bad? You just slept the whole day."

"I don't want to see your face. I don't want to see the room, the window. I don't want to see this stuff."

"I'll go get a doctor. First, you need to eat this though. A cup of tea, mashed potatoes, chicken, boiled carrots, green jello . . . Fancy stuff."

"Get me the doctor now."

"The doctor is not due for another hour or so."

"I'll check myself out."

"You're not well enough. You're admitted as an involuntary, besides. Once you're medically stable, you will be transferred to another hospital. Perhaps tomorrow. Depending on how you do."

"Who decided this?"

"The doctors. Your father."

"He can't decide for me!"

"Listen, you need it. You were practically dead when they got you here."

"I'm still dying."

"Meanwhile, you're alive."

"Every time I try to kick off, I find you there, trying to save me. I don't want to be saved. Don't you get it? Leave me alone now. Take the tray with you."

"You want to change that gown?"

"Yeah."

"Here, let me wipe off that sweat. See you later. Someone else takes the tray. Just leave it there."

Ben will remain in a half-seated position, looking at the tray on the side of his bed, surprised by a feeling of growing hunger. He will begin to eat slowly, sipping the lukewarm tea. Darkness will have wiped away the view of the green forest and the skyline framed by his window, leaving behind street lights twinkling anonymously between illuminated office towers. He will have one more night in the world where seeing life and its nauseating colours will not be required of his wide open eyes.

ᐸᐳ

John wakes up from his day sleep, the afternoon still ahead of him, its possibilities unborn. He lies in bed remembering the dream from the day before, the hummed lullaby in the sea, the familiar voice he was unable to name. He rises, thinking of Selma's white slipper in the dusty brown suitcase in the furnace room. He passes by the window, glancing through it at the yellow door. The sky is dark grey, the trees, bright green. The door is only partially visible behind the opaque undulating crown of a tree on the sidewalk. A light blue plastic pouch stuffed with flyers hangs from its bronze handle. September comes down the street and approaches the door, her hips swaying hesitantly over high heeled shoes, the peach-coloured skirt falling around her knees like a wilted lily. Eric lags behind, his red packsack bouncing on his shoulders as he skips and hops towards the door. She enters and calls the boy, who makes her wait while he jumps a few more times over an imaginary line. John sees her lips moving. The boy looks at her, shrugs his shoulders and walks towards her slowly, his head bent down. The door closes.

John turns away from his window and goes to the furnace room. He approaches the dusty brown suitcase on the floor. He unbuckles it and drags it into his living room. The dust makes him sneeze. He takes a tea towel and wipes the suitcase clean, then opens it and removes the only object inside, the slipper, now yellowed, its feathery bow flattened. The small pointy heel was rounded by use long ago. John sits on his couch, slipper in hand. Whoever she was then, she no longer is, he reflects, looking at it dispassionately. Her middle toe was slightly longer than the others, and it curved down. On the inside of her left thigh was a small birthmark in the shape of Madagascar. Has anyone else given it a name? He places the solitary slipper on his desk among notebooks and bills, beside the jade statue of a forever smiling Buddha, which she had given him as a goodbye gift. It had sat in the window of a gift shop at the airport. They had been spending time looking at the display windows along the large sunny side of the airport lounge during a long uncomfortable wait in which what had to be said had remained unspoken. The voice on the speakers calling passengers to the gate brusquely ended the long drawn out silence entrapping them. She hurried into the shop to get the Buddha and shoved the plastic bag with the statue into his hands as he rushed off towards his flight. He turned around and saw her standing, waving mechanically. Then she disappeared.

It was an hour later, in the cabin, that the grief hit him. Like a man about to vomit, he rushed to the bathroom, clutching the plastic bag with the Buddha. His sobbing came out in an uncontrollable fit. All at once he was letting go of the small boy looking for a father, the child struggling to make himself small and weightless so his mother wouldn't dislike him, he was abandoning his dead friend who had been tortured, he was grieving the loss of his beloved blue sea, he was deserting Madagascar, the soft warm spot inside Selma's thigh, his secret island. All that was left was a strange little statue of Buddha in a plastic bag in his fingers, and his thumping heart and his sorrow somewhere above the clouds. Somewhere at the end of this trip was the stranger he would become. He rinsed his face and remained standing in the narrow washroom until he felt capable of returning to his seat.

He realizes he has been standing in the middle of his living room clasping the Buddha in one hand and the slipper in the other. He has a couple of hours' time before returning to work. He places the objects back on his desk and retrieves a white handkerchief from his dresser drawer. He opens it up and places inside it the two objects, along with Salvador's discarded keys, and ties the four corners together into one tight knot. He puts on his jacket and leaves the apartment, crossing Carré St-Louis with its water-spewing fountain and festive flowers, walking downhill towards Old Montreal, until he reaches the waterfront. He spends a few minutes gazing at the wide, rippling river, its currents moving in incomprehensible directions. He reaches for the shapeless white bundle in his packsack and throws it in. It hits the murky waters with a quick splash before being swallowed into the invisible depths. He imagines it falling slowly towards the sticky riverbed, making a small dent on the soft clay bottom.

John walks away from the waterfront and crosses the street. He feels light inside, almost giddy, watching the play of the afternoon sun upon the shimmering maple saplings lining the street, in postcard-perfect Old Montreal with its tidy shops selling Inuit art and dreamcatchers. He walks on Saint Sulpice siding the Notre Dame Basilica, and is about to cross Rue Notre Dame when he hears the screeching of tires very close to his ears, and the thick sudden noise of impact, and feels sharp pain at the back of his head as his limbs crumble and his own scream echoes in his ears. His last impression is of grey rough concrete and the bright carmine colour of his own blood oozing over it. He closes his eyes and feels the air moving about his face, the slow flapping of large wings beside him like sails hit by violent winds; hovering above the world he sees the roof of the Basilica and the small crumpled body beside the church as a crowd gathers, and the siren of an ambulance gets closer and louder, and he glides above and away, a creature unattached to earth and its movements.

Epilogue

Dear Selma,

My name is Pablo. I was a good friend of John's in Montreal. I gather you were his girlfriend a long time ago. I'm sorry to have to announce his passing to you. He died recently, in a traffic accident. I'm very grieved to be contacting you under such circumstances.

John was an extremely private man. He had many friends; yet, no one really knew much about him, or the circumstances that brought him to Montreal. He was kindness personified. In fact, he worked as a nurse in a hospital here, on night shift. Although he never mentioned you to me, I discovered your existence in the pages of his green notebook which I've enclosed in this package along with some photographs and objects you may find of interest. I felt this book needed to find its way to you because it seems you never left his mind. I did not come across any sign of siblings or extended family among his belongings. His mother passed away, and he apparently never knew his father. At the time of his death, he was not married and I know of no other attachments. Perhaps he was looking for a way to contact you. I found some dusty telephone directories from various Swedish cities in one of his closets.

I have written my telephone number and email address at the bottom of this letter in case you would like to contact me.

With my kindest regards,

Pablo Mendes